# ALIEN ABDUCTION FOR UNICORNS

## THE INTERGALACTIC GUIDE TO HUMANS

SKYE MACKINNON

Peryton Press

Cover by Peryton Covers.

Published by Peryton Press.

skyemackinnon.com

# CONTENTS

## A NOTE ON UNICORNS
### BY THOLIN, SON OF THALIN

I t is a well-known fact across the universe that unicorns are real. They have many names, ranging from the simple (onehorn, horn-beast, solohorn) to the comical (stabhorn, glitter-pain).

Only on a few backwater planets do people doubt their existence. One of those planets is Peritus, known by locals as Earth, Erde, земля́, Terre and other names in their copious languages.[1]

It is not established why Peritans refuse to believe in unicorns. This will need further research.

# LESSON 1

# HOW TO TAME A UNICORN

# LESSON 1: HOW TO TAME A UNICORN

BRUIN

The sharp horn narrowly missed my throat, but one of the hooves found its mark. I repressed a scream as pain shot through my shin and up my leg. Only years of experience kept me from making the fatal mistake of crying out. Loud noise would only upset the stabhorn further.

"Easy, girl," I muttered soothingly while staying out of reach of the deadly horn. My voice was tense with pain, but I hoped she wouldn't notice. "Calm down."

The mare didn't listen. She reared up again, her hooves coming perilously close to crushing my skull. An'tia was huge for her age and gender. I barely reached up to the lowest point of her back. With a furious whinny, she landed on all fours again. Golden mist rose from her nostrils, a sign of her anger and fear.

"Take it easy. I'm not here to hurt you."

9

An'tia didn't care. She glared at me with her azure blue eyes, her disdain and wrath evident. She was going to be a handful. Every new arrival at the sanctuary was scared, dangerous and unpredictable, but her size set her aside from the other stabhorns. I wasn't a small male, not in the slightest, but next to her, I felt tiny.

Her hooves scraped across the ground as she got ready to attack again. The golden mist coming from her nostrils surrounded her like a cloud, shimmering in the evening light of the Second Sun. Maybe it was time to give her some space and try again tomorrow.

An'tia pointed her horn at my heart, the tip dark with dried blood. The blood was green, probably from one of the Quurkat traders who'd transported her on their ship. I hoped they'd sought medical attention. An'tia was a venom-tipped stabhorn, a rare breed whose horns were coated in a slow-acting poison. If the injured traders didn't take the antidote, they'd be paralysed within three intergalactic hours.

With a snort, An'tia shook her mane, her horn still pointing at my chest. It was time to retreat and give her some space.

Very slowly, I backed away. My injured leg hurt when I put weight on it, but I managed to keep from wincing in pain. I'd head to the nearest medpod as soon as I'd written a report on this first encounter.

An'tia whinnied, but stayed in place as she watched my withdrawal. I kept eye contact with her to show the stabhorn that I wasn't prey. I wasn't giving up,

I was just taking a break. I'd be back and return again and again until she was ready to trust me.

And then everything happened at once. Someone shouted from behind me. I stumbled. And An'tia charged.

Blinding pain exploded in my chest. Blue eyes met mine. An'tia's triumphant gaze was the last thing I saw before darkness and pain overwhelmed me.

I FLOATED *on a river of golden hair. It swept around me, enveloping me in a soothing embrace that washed away all memory of pain. I let the river take me, too weak to resist the steady current. Above me, a blue sky was dappled with fluffy white clouds unlike I'd never seen before. The blue reminded me of something, but the thought was carried away by the river before I could grasp it.*

*I didn't know how long I drifted. A deep feeling of harmony and peace filled me. I was content simply to float and let the river carry me. The destination didn't matter.*

*Over time, the clouds above me became larger until they drowned out almost all the blue. Even after they'd hidden the sky, they continued to grow, expanding downwards. When the closest one was only an arm's length away from me, I tried to swim away from it, but my limbs got tangled in the hair. I was trapped. Helpless, I could do nothing but watch as the clouds grew. A strange scent reached my nose, spicy and exotic. Was that what clouds smelled like? And then a voice echoed through the whiteness, a female, speaking in a melodic language I couldn't understand. But then the cloud touching me solidified, pressing against my face-*

"STOP STRUGGLING."

A familiar voice made me stop immediately. I was used to following his orders. My sire.

I opened my eyes. As always, it was as if looking into a mirror. A mirror that showed me what I would look like forty rotations from now. My sire had the same angular face, the same piercing purple eyes, the same curved ears that seemed too large for my head. He had a few wrinkles around his eyes that I lacked, but otherwise, we were identical. Not surprising considering I was his clone.

"You barely made it," he said with a sigh. Disappointment swung in his words. Not because I'd almost died. Because I almost destroyed his legacy. He'd paid a small fortune to have me created, yet I'd not given him what he'd expected in return. It didn't matter that I'd become the best stabhorn tamer on the planet. It didn't matter that I was happy with my life. No, to my sire, I was a constant source of disappointment.

"How bad is it?" I asked, then coughed. My throat was dry, but my sire didn't offer me a drink. He simply stared down at me with an unreadable expression.

"They had to give you an organ transplant or you wouldn't have survived."

Wow. I'd really come close then. I'd been wounded by stabhorns before, it was almost part of the job description, but I'd never been hurt this badly.

"I gave permission to have the credits deducted from your account," my sire continued. "But since you've clearly not handled your money well, you're now in debt."

I wasn't surprised he'd not offered to pay for my operation with his own credits. He'd always told me that creating me had been expensive enough. I'd had to work for my living from the moment I was old enough.

Debt. Great. I wondered how long it would take me to pay back the credits. Being a stabhorn tamer came with a lot of prestige, but the salary was way below what my sire earned in his job as a Professor at the Intergalactic University.

"Where's my Commband?" I asked weakly.

He handed it to me and waited while I pulled up my bank balance. I cursed when I saw the amount, then closed my eyes in denial. It would take decades.

My sire clicked his tongue in disapproval. "You know you shouldn't use such language. It doesn't befit your status."

"Status?" I laughed humourlessly. "I'm bankrupt. How am I even going to pay for my food? Or my electricity?"

"It was your decision to play with dangerous

13

animals. You shouldn't be surprised that you got hurt. It's been a long time coming, if you ask me."

"I'm not asking you," I snapped. I tried to sit up, but a wave of dizziness crashed over me. I let myself drop back onto the medpod's soft mattress.

"There is one way you could make up for it," my sire said, a twisted smirk around his lips. Oh no. I wasn't going to like this. "You could come work for me."

I couldn't repress a laugh. "Work for you? I'd rather be gouged by a stabhorn again."

"That could be arranged," he said coldly. "I will send you the details later. Once they evict you, I'm sure you will reconsider."

He left before I could say another word. I was seething, desperate to punch something. How had my life suddenly become a nightmare? Yesterday, I'd been the darling of the stabhorn scene. Today, I was injured, poor and miserable.

AFTER TWO ROTATIONS in the medical centre, I was discharged home. My landlord didn't know yet that I was bankrupt, so I was able to stay here for a bit longer. Only when I couldn't pay the next rent would she discover the truth. I'd spent the past two rotations trying to get a loan to carry me over, but my medical data hat already updated and nobody would lend money to someone who'd almost died and had only just been released from the medical centre. They said I could try again in twenty rotations, but by then, I'd starved.

I opened the cool locker and wrinkled my nose at the rotten smell emanating from it. Most of my food had gone off while I'd been away. I'd been in an induced coma for eight rotations while I recovered from the transplant. This was one of the moments that I wished I had a mate. Someone to look after me while I was sick. Someone to replenish the cool locker. Someone to hug me and heal the hurt my sire's behaviour had caused. Not that I would ever admit that to anyone. My public image was that of a playboy who had no intentions of ever settling down. In reality, I craved the stability a mate could provide. The females I occasionally took home only fulfilled my physical urges. They didn't block the loneliness.

The main console blinked, signalling unread messages. I dropped into my favourite massage pod and told the AI to read me my messages. With a groan, I relaxed as dozens of hands seemed to massage my tired body. I'd missed my pod.

The first two messages were from friends asking how I was. How nice. Not that they were actual friends. They were friends with my money and fame. Now that one of those was gone, would they stick around? I doubted it.

The third message was from my sire. I was tempted to delete it before listening, but as always, I felt a tiny glimmer of hope that my sire might say something nice to me.

For the first time in his life.

"...spoken to the Dean. She's agreed to fund a research project involving Peritans."

I rolled my eyes. They were my sire's favourite alien species. Peritans lived on some backwater planet and hadn't even travelled further than their own moon, but they'd grown to fame across the universe in the past decade. The Intergalactic University was mostly to blame for that. My sire had been one of the first researchers to look into Peritan culture, a contrast to most of his colleagues who were more interested in their biology and intellect. For some strange reason, Peritans were sexually compatible with most sentient species. It made them extremely valuable, even though they likely weren't aware of it. That's why a blockade had been put around their planet and the IGU was the only institution with abduction rights.

My sire loved Peritans more than his own offspring, that much had been clear to me for years. Him mentioning that at the beginning of his message was yet more evidence of that painful fact.

"...you and a stabhorn."

I sat up straight. What? Lost in thought, I'd missed part of the message, so I had the AI rewind.

"...can find stabhorns all over Peritan mythology, but they have stopped believing in their existence. I want to find out why. That's why I got funding to send you and a stabhorn. You'll abduct some natives and confront them with the stabhorn to study their reaction. For legal reasons, it will be best to bring them here rather than do the research on their planet."

My sire had gone crazy. He wanted me to take a stabhorn to Peritus? I had better things to do. Besides, stabhorn hated space travel. They needed fresh air and solid ground beneath their hooves.

"Your salary will cover your medical debts and then some," the message continued. "You'll be able to resume your lavish lifestyle after your return."

Despite the AI's monotonous voice, I could almost hear my sire's disapproving tone. He saw my life as a stabhorn tamer as wasted potential.

"Let me know your decision within the next cycle. I have already spoken to your employers and they've agreed to lend me a stabhorn named An'tia."

I snorted. I bet they didn't tell him that An'tia was the stabhorn who'd almost killed me. She was the worst possible choice for a long space journey.

I was tempted to tell my sire to klat off and stick his research into where the suns didn't shine. But the thought of An'tia made me reconsider. She deserved to be accompanied by someone who knew her, not some stranger.

The massage pod helped me make up my mind. I'd lose it if I didn't do this. I'd lose everything. How bad could a trip to Peritus get?

# LESSON 2

# FIRST CONTACT

## LESSON 2: FIRST CONTACT

TARA

"Why aren't you wearing a kilt?" a lady asked me, disapproval radiating from her.

"Only the men do." I resisted the urge to roll my eyes. I got this question almost every day.

"But you'd look so much more Scottish with a kilt."

Tourists. I hated them so much. Yet it was my job to keep them happy.

I forced a sweet smile. "I'll pass your feedback on to my manager. Now, are there any other questions before we finish this tour?"

The same woman raised her hand, a challenge blazing in her dark eyes. "Do you play the bagpipes? We were promised bagpipes."

My colleague Tim rescued me before I could resort to murder. He waved a stack of postcards at the group of mostly elderly well-to-dos. "Grab a postcard, everyone; there's a discount code for the shop printed on the back. You'll find some wonderful souvenirs in our shop, including kilts and bagpipes."

He winked at me, knowing my pain all too well. He'd been doing this job longer than me. With his red curls, green eyes and MacCallum kilt, he looked Scottish enough to satisfy the tourists, but as soon as he opened his mouth and revealed his Canadian accent, they looked at him as if he'd personally betrayed them.

I half-heartedly waved goodbye at my group and headed back into the castle. Behind the shop was a crammed wee room for us tour guides to hang out. Someone had made a pot of tea and it was still lukewarm. I poured myself a cup and collapsed on an uncomfortable wooden chair that looked right at home in this medieval castle.

My legs ached from walking and standing all day. Only one more tour, then I could head home.

"Any coffee left?"

Sharon poked her head into the room. She was the senior guide who'd trained me all those years ago. Back when I'd thought I'd only do this job for a season and then travel the world. Yeah, right.

"Nope, but there's lukewarm tea."

"Nah, thanks. I'll make more coffee instead. I've got a planning meeting in twenty minutes and I bet it's going to last at least two hours. I need proper caffeine."

I bit back a comment about how tea contained caffeine as well. I knew Sharon was teasing me. We'd had this discussion many times, the friendly argument between a tea and a coffee addict.

"What's the meeting about?" I asked while she busied herself with the coffee machine.

"Unicorns. Yeah, you heard that right. Someone at Head Office had the brilliant idea to stick some horns on horses. They've been trialling it at Edinburgh Castle and the kids loved it, so now they want to send them here, too."

"Do they look halfway realistic?"

"Maybe if you're a four-year-old." Sharon chuckled. "Two of the unicorns will be here tomorrow for a photo op. I think you did the social media posts for the Mary Queen of Scots exhibition, right? Want to do the same for the unicorns?"

That sounded a whole lot better than leading entitled tourists through the castle all day. "Sounds good. I'll bring my proper camera tomorrow."

Sharon plopped onto the chair next to me, exhaustion lining her face. "Maybe stick to your phone. That way, it might not be as obvious that the horns are made from cardboard."

I LOVED ARRIVING at the castle at sunrise. The hills in the distance were painted a hundred shades of orange and red, while the castle walls themselves glinted golden. I imagined what people hundreds of years would have thought of that sight. A golden castle, proof that the royal line was indeed appointed by God.

One of the security guards had unlocked the gates, but I was the first guide to arrive. I'd always been a morning person, so this wasn't unusual. I enjoyed experiencing the castle during this quiet time. History seemed to seep from the walls, waiting to be acknowledged by anyone who would listen. Later, it would be too loud to really soak in the atmosphere. It was kind of sad that the tourists only got half the experience of visiting the castle. Being surrounded by others, hearing a dozen different languages and the sounds of modern life, distracted from the true essence of being in a historic place.

I made a big pot of tea and poured myself the second cup of the day. It would be one of many more. A loud yawn announced Tim before he entered the guides' room, looking as if he'd barely slept.

"How do you look so awake?" he grumbled. "It's not fair."

"Long night?"

"Terry took me to the opera in Glasgow. We missed the last train, so we slept at the station. The first train was at 4am, so I've had about an hour's actual sleep in my bed. Terry's shift doesn't start until noon, so the bastard gets to snooze while I have to work."

While he continued complaining, I handed him a mug. "You stay here and get some rest. I'll put up the signs."

Tim shot me a grateful but tired look. "You sure?"

"I owe you for saving me from that group yesterday."

He grinned. "That's what colleagues are there for."

I gulped down a few sips of hot tea, burning my throat yet too impatient to wait for it to cool down, then collected the signs from the shop. They displayed the castle's opening times and entry prices, although I doubted the point of them. Visitors would usually ask about both at the ticket office even though the signs were right in front of them.

Heaving the heavy wooden signs to the front gates, I noticed a lone man standing next to a horse at the other end of the parking lot. Hadn't Sharon mentioned two unicorns? Maybe one had lost its horn.

With the sun behind him, their silhouettes were dark against the morning light, looking almost magical. I pulled out my phone and took a quick picture, then quickly set up the signs before I forgot.

The guy stayed in place, waiting for me to approach. His horse was huge, towering above him. I knew nothing about horses, but this one seemed exceedingly tall. Maybe they'd chosen it especially for the unicorn gig, since that would make it even more imposing when surrounded by small children.

Up close, the horse was even larger. I'd underestimated how tall the man next to it was. I wasn't small, but next to him, I felt tiny. His shoulders were broad, his black t-shirt too tight for his muscular arms. He either had a job other than chaperoning fake unicorns or worked out every day. I blinked against the sun, trying to make out his features. He was bald; not a look I usually liked, but it only made him seem more attractive.

I chastised myself for letting my thoughts stray that way. I was here in a professional capacity. Maybe I was about to get my period. That always messed with my hormones and turned me into a cat in heat.

"Are you here for the photoshoot?" I asked. "Wait, don't answer that. I don't think we're going to get any other unicorns visiting us today."

My mouth was running away from me. Think before you speak, Tara. But he was making me nervous. He was intimidating and attractive and looking at me way too intensely. His gaze swept over me from top to bottom, as if he was ingraining every detail into memory. I felt strangely naked under his gaze.

I forced myself to focus on the horse. It was safer than to risk meeting his eyes and get drawn into their depths.

"That horn looks really realistic," I blurted. "I assumed it would be a cardboard roll or something silly like that, but this is beautiful. How do you make it shimmer that way?"

The horse snorted, hot steam rising from its nostrils. Its fur was a silvery white all over, reflecting the morning sun. Its large eyes were a stunning turquoise framed with silver lashes. The mane looked freshly brushed and a few golden ribbons had been tied into it. I wondered if the guy had done that or someone else. He didn't look the type to care much about ribbons.

The horn was a curved spire of silver and gold. I couldn't quite determine what material it was made from. Definitely not plastic. It reminded me of mother-of-pearl, but that couldn't be right. How was it even attached? I couldn't see any cords. Surely they hadn't glued it on? That would be cruel.

I wanted to reach out and touch the horn, but the huge horse was intimidating. It stared at me just like I'd stared at the fake unicorn. Its eyes sparked with intelligence. I'd never been around horses much, but I was starting to feel like this horse was special.

"You can touch her," the man answered my unspoken question. He had a slight accent, but it was barely noticeable.

"Sure she won't bite?"

"She won't bite *you*."

I faked a smile, not sure if he was making a joke.

"Does she bite other people?"

"Sometimes. She stabbed me once. I almost died."

Alright, he had to be joking. That horn was fake and couldn't be hard enough to stab someone.

I turned to look at him and realised his intense gaze was still fixed on me. "Are you making fun of me?"

"Never."

He said it with such conviction that I didn't doubt him in the slightest. Everything about him was intense. His huge body, his dark eyes that seemed almost black, every word that came from his perfectly shaped lips. Lips that looked very kissable indeed.

I took a step back to get some distance between us. This situation was becoming ever stranger. I should take them into the castle and start taking some pictures. For some reason, I didn't want to stay alone with him any longer. Not because he was making me uncomfortable. Because he was making me feel too comfortable.

"Follow me," I said and turned around before I could change my mind. "There's a great spot in the Queen Anne Garden where you can see the castle looming up above. And after that, we can go into the inner courtyard for some pictures in front of the Royal Palace."

The horse's hooves click-clacked over the cobblestone, but the man's steps were silent. I was tempted to look over my shoulder to make sure he was following me.

The security guard by the gate stared at us, his eyes wide. "That unicorn looks very real," he muttered to me. "I didn't know horses could be that big."

I shrugged and waited until he lifted the barrier that prevented cars from driving into the castle complex. Something warm touched my shoulder, followed by a burst of hot air against the side of my face.

"Turn very slowly," the stranger said, his voice calm. "No sudden movements."

I did as instructed, coming face to face with the

unicorn. She kept her muzzle on my shoulder. Something akin to humour twinkled in her turquoise eyes, but I had to imagine that.

"Reach up and stroke her cheek. She likes that."

I gingerly rubbed the soft fur beneath the horse's eye. She snorted and pushed against my hand as if to ask for more.

"I'll take a picture," the guard announced. "You two look adorable together."

I frowned. I didn't want to be called that. The horse was adorable, yes, despite her intimidating size, but not me.

Without warning, her tongue shot out and licked my ear. Yuck.

"Can I step away from her now?" I asked the horse's owner, realising at the same time that I didn't even know his name. I'd forgotten all about polite introductions. That wasn't professional at all. I was representing not just the castle team, but all of Historic Scotland, the charity looking after many of Scotland's ancient sites. I had to get my act together and stop being so affected by the stranger's presence.

"Slowly, don't startle her. She likes you."

Great. I stroked her warm cheek one last time, then stepped back. She inclined her head a little, then snorted happily. At least that's how I interpreted it.

"I'll send you the pictures later," the guard promised.

I probably wouldn't take him up on that. I hated

seeing pictures of myself. I preferred to be behind the camera where I could indulge my insecurities.

Now that the barrier was up, I led the stranger and the horse through the gate and up the uneven cobblestone path until we got to the gardens. The roses were in their final days of bloom and their sweet fragrance filled the air. It was one of my favourite parts of the castle complex.

Ignoring the 'don't step on the grass' signs, I headed to the wall looming high above us. When I stopped to make sure they'd followed me onto the grass, I wasn't surprised to have the stranger stare at me intensely once again.

"That beech tree over there is over two hundred years old," I said, falling into my tour guide routine. "And did you know that Queen Anne, after whom this garden is named, never actually visited the castle?"

"I did not know that," the man said, an amused smirk twisting his lips. "And there's something else I don't know. Your name."

"Tara. Tara Crawford."

He touched two fingers to his forehead and gave me a short bow. "Bruin, son of Tholin."

Again, I felt like he was making fun of me, yet his expression was sincere. I couldn't make head nor toe of this man.

He stroked the horse's mane, getting a soft whinny in response. "And this is An'tia. She is as pleased to meet you as I am."

The unicorn stared at me. Her turquoise eyes

seemed to turn into swirling whirlpools, pulling me in. Unseen ropes wrapped around my chest, restricting my breathing. My knees buckled, yet I couldn't look away from those gorgeous eyes. I was trapped, held in place by a force I had no words to describe. My body was frozen, yet my mind was free as I floated towards the unicorn, pulled into the depths of her soul.

# LESSON 3

# INTRODUCING YOURSELF TO YOUR ABDUCTEE

# LESSON 3: INTRODUCING YOURSELF TO YOUR ABDUCTEE

BRUIN

As soon as my mate was unconscious, I picked her up and pressed her close against my chest. I'd been craving to touch her the moment I'd laid eyes on her, but I'd not want to scare her. Fumbling for my C-Band, I took a quick look around to make sure nobody was watching, then pressed the button. Bright light enveloped us. An'tia whinnied in annoyance, then her hooves hit the floor of my spaceship. She huffed, angry to be back in the confined space.

We'd been on Peritus for five of their sun rotations. The trip here had been long and uneventful, but the moment we'd broken through the planet's atmosphere, An'tia had begun to glitter. Her white coat had sparkled as if she'd been doused in pure starlight. I'd never seen anything more beautiful.

What irony that the only reason I'd come to Peritus

was because of my father. I bet he'd regret persuading me to do this once he found out that An'tia had found my mate. Not just any mate. My *soul*mate.

While An'tia's glittering fur was a clear sign that my mate was somewhere on the planet, there'd been no way of knowing where until we'd set foot on what the natives called Earth. At first, we'd landed on the wrong continent, but An'tia had guided me all the way to a small country the natives called Scotland. It was a beautiful place that reminded me a little of Allopo, my home planet. Although it would take me some time to get used to only having one sun light up the sky.

On the way, I'd dutifully made notes of how the Peritans reacted to An'tia. Most smiled when they saw her or wanted to take something they called *selfies*. Others wanted to touch her horn and desired to find out what it was made of. An'tia didn't let any of them touch her, but she was surprisingly docile and didn't use her venom on anyone.

We finally found my mate in front of an old structure that didn't look fit to live in. Maybe it was her family's estate, but she lacked the funds to repair it. I'd expected my mate to be confused by An'tia, but she'd looked at us as if she'd expected me to arrive with a stabhorn. My father assumed that Peritans didn't believe in the existence of stabhorns, but there was a chance he was wrong. My mate certainly hadn't looked at An'tia as if she was a mythical beast.

A gong sounded, signalling that the beaming process had been completed and all our atoms had been reassembled in the correct order. I hurried over to the medpod and gently lay my mate inside. She was still unconscious, but her breathing was steady. Her golden hair spread around her head like a veil. It reminded me of something, a distant memory, but I couldn't remember why her beautiful hair looked so familiar.

I activated the medpod and started a full diagnostic sequence. I'd been told beaming was safe for Peritans, but I wanted to make sure. As much as the Intergalactic University had researched their species in the past decade or so, there was still a lot to learn about Peritans. I grinned when I realised I'd get an up-close introduction to their peculiar manners. My sire had told me stories of their habits, which seemed to involve a lot of shaking hands and speaking in riddles, but he'd only been to Peritus twice. Most of his research was based on going through their literature. He'd become fascinated by their fiction and written several papers on the surprising realism in a genre they called 'monster romance'. Now that I had a Peritan mate, I regretted that I didn't pay more attention to my sire's research. But I wouldn't give him the satisfaction by asking him for advice. No way.

The medpod's screen filled with data. She had no translation implant fitted, so I instructed the pod to inject her with a basic one. Mine was more advanced, letting me speak alien languages as well as understand them, but it was a more invasive procedure. I didn't want to subject her to that without her consent. For now, a simple synthetic ear slug implant that would translate whatever she heard would suffice.

My female's iron levels were too low, but everything else seemed normal for her species. The medpod calculated that she was twenty-seven Peritus rotations young. That seemed barely old enough to be out of diapers. Had I abducted a youngling?!

Cold fear gripped my heart. I'd be in so much trouble. And I'd have to wait for decades for her to grow up until she could truly become my mate. I wouldn't survive that long.

I changed the medpod's unit setting to intergalactic standards. Ah, that made more sense. She was only two IG years younger than me. Thank the stars. I could mate with her. At the thought of being with her, becoming true soulmates by completing the sacred starlight ritual, my cocks hardened.

Wait. *Both* cocks. That was a strange new sensation. My mating cock had been dormant in its sleeve, but now that I'd found my mate, I supposed it was time for it to awaken. I reached for my crotch, then thought better of it. If Tara woke up now, I didn't want me touching myself to be the first thing she saw.

I distracted myself by scrolling through the data in front of me. Her left arm had been broken in the past and the bone had regrown at a slight angle. I instructed the medpod to heal it properly. Hopefully, my mate hadn't been in pain because of her species' primitive medicine.

One other notification confused me. There was a

foreign body inside her uterus. I zoomed in, dreading what I was about to see. Did she have a parasite? Or worse, had someone conducted experiments on her?

The object resembled a small stick with two arms and a string hanging from the other end. How very peculiar. It didn't send out any signals and it looked simple enough to be of Peritan origin. Why would she have a stick in her uterus? Did she even know about it? I had the medpod remove it just in case. I didn't want my mate to suffer. I'd have to ask her later if she was aware of the device.

Satisfied that she was in good health otherwise, I ended the medpod sequence. It asked me if I wanted her to regain consciousness. For a moment, I hesitated. I enjoyed looking at her, taking in her alien beauty. Once she woke, she'd have questions. I'd have to explain why she was no longer on her planet. She'd been surprisingly calm when confronted with An'tia, so maybe I was worrying over nothing. She might be glad to be away from her planet. Glad to be with her soulmate.

An'tia whinnied from behind me. I sometimes worried that she could read my thoughts. She was too intelligent and intuitive for a stabhorn, even a venom-tipped one. At least she'd decided I was a friend. The first few days of our journey had been rough. She'd almost stabbed me a second time. It took all my experience and patience to get her to trust me. Stabhorns bonded for life, so now that she'd decided I was worth her company, she'd stay with me for as long as she lived. Or until she found her own mate. She was still young and it would be a few more IG years until she started to develop the urge to search for her mate.

I looked back at my own female. She was so perfect. Smaller than the females of my own kind, but there was an inner strength to her, even while she was sleeping.

An'tia stepped closer, her hooves echoing on the hard metal floor. She was going to wake Tara with the same stabhorn magic that had made her unconscious.

"Wait," I told her quickly. "Let's get her into more comfortable surroundings first."

I gently lifted Tara into my arms. She was so light, so small. I was strangely scared of holding her too tightly, of squeezing her to death. Her scent was spicy and alluring, reminding me of the laotus flower which only bloomed when both suns were at their strongest. I breathed in deep. Tara smelled familiar. Like home. We'd only just met, but I could already imagine us growing old together. We'd have a family. Many younglings, born naturally, not grown in a lab like myself. We'd have our own stabhorn park., far away from overeager fans. And-

I bumped my head at the door leading to the relaxation quarter. Every. Single. Time. The ship belonged to the IGU and clearly wasn't made for a male of my size. I bet my sire had hired this one on purpose to make me uncomfortable. My forehead would have permanent dents by the time we got back home.

Just like the rest of the ship, the relaxation room was small, well-used yet clean. As soon as we entered, a narrow bench descended from the walls and a table rose from the floor.

"Andromeda, adjust the settings to two passengers," I told the ship's AI. A second bench was lowered from the wall. It would be comfortable for Tara, but for me, it was only wide enough for half my buttocks. Until now, I'd spent most of the time on the bridge, where the captain's chair was more suitable for my stature, and in the cargo bay with An'tia. But since the relaxation quarter was the least intimidating-looking part of the ship, it seemed like a good idea to wake Tara in here.

I carefully laid her on one of the benches before brushing her hair out of her face. Again, the golden hair reminded me of something. I'd figure it out eventually.

She looked so peaceful. I shouldn't wake her yet. But that was cowardice speaking. I'd have to face her questions eventually. I remembered the manual my sire had given me and which sat unread in my inbox. I activated the holo display on my C-Band and pulled up the book. *The Intergalactic University's Guide to Humans* by Professor Katila. My sire had mentioned her. She'd been a catalyst in introducing Peritus to the IGU's alien species department, but had eventually gone mad. During a breakdown, she'd threatened the lives of a Peritan female and her Kardarian mates. Three of them. I was glad I didn't have to share my own mate. I just hoped I'd be enough to satisfy her. I'd heard Peritan females were voracious when it came to mating.

I had a lot of experience, but only with my pleasure cock. With her, it would be the first time I released my mating cock from its sleeve. It wasn't something I could practise. It would happen during the starlight ritual, when we formed our everlasting bond.

Until today, I'd never thought much about my mating cock, but now that it had awoken, the sleeve around it felt tight and uncomfortable. I wanted relief, but I knew only my mate could release it from the sleeve. If I tried, it would hurt and might damage it forever. Not a risk I'd take. I'd just have to convince her to mate with me soon.

To distract myself from the discomfort, I navigated to chapter 3, *Introducing Yourself to Your Abductee*.

"Keep in mind that your Abductee has just been ripped from their native habitat. They will be scared and confused. At the time of writing, Peritus is not a member of the Galactic Council and most of its inhabitants are unaware of the presence of life beyond their planet. For them, you will be the alien, not them. Be patient and gentle. Avoid loud noises that might startle them.

"If your physical form is very different from Peritans (they are a bipedal species but start their life as tetrapods), consider wearing a disguise during your First Contact Experience (FCE). Don't overwhelm them with too much information at once, it might be more than their fragile minds can handle.

"Start by introducing yourself. Don't go into too much detail. Reassure them that you have no intentions to eat/kill/hurt/probe/... them. The recommended IGU strategy is to conduct the FCE in your space vehicle while still in orbit around Peritus. We have found it helps to show Abductees their planet in order to speed up their acceptance of their circumstances.

"Once they feel comfortable in your presence, remove your disguise. Remember to take it slow. Overwhelmed Peritans have been known to scream hysterically, rock back and forth, whimper and even leak from their eyes. Try and avoid this at any cost. You may be tempted to sedate your Abductee to make it easier for yourself. Don't. It will lengthen the FCE and could risk your future Abductor-Abductee-relationship."

I swallowed hard. This sounded more difficult that I'd imagined. I should have read the book before now.

"Andromeda, create a virtual viewscreen and display our external view of Peritus."

A digital window appeared on the wall opposite the benches. The blue-and-green planet filled it almost entirely. I'd seen prettier planets, but it wasn't one of the ugliest. In fact, the little moon was adorable. One sun, one moon. I liked the symmetry of it.

But I was stalling.

It was time to wake my mate.

# LESSON 4
# ANGER
# MANAGEMENT FOR
# ABDUCTEES

# LESSON 4: ANGER MANAGEMENT FOR ABDUCTEES

TARA

I dreamed that I was riding a unicorn. I knew it was a dream from the start, but that didn't stop me from enjoying the experience. We were flying high above the clouds, rainbows shimmering all around us. I gripped the unicorn's silver mane, but I knew I was safe on her broad back even without a saddle. She wouldn't let me fall.

From up here, I had the most spectacular view of the world below. The clouds were semi-translucent, giving me a glimpse of the land we were flying over. The colours seemed strange to me, even for a dream. Instead of green grass or blue water, everything was held in golden and orange hues. Even the ocean was a deep ochre.

We flew higher and higher until the clouds were only small flecks of silver fluff. The unicorn whinnied, *pure joy reverberating in the ethereal sound. I laughed and hugged her neck. She whinnied again, this time louder, so loud that it rang in my ears and-*

I opened my eyes, suddenly wide awake as if I'd really heard that neigh. It only took me a fraction of a second to recall what had happened. I'd stared into the horse's eyes and that was the last thing I remembered. I must have fainted.

I was inside now, but before I could see more of my surroundings, Bruin leaned over me, his dark eyes filled with concern.

"How are you feeling?"

"Fine, I think. What happened?" My throat was dry. How long had I been asleep?

"An'tia thought this was the kindest way. I apologise on her behalf."

His words made no sense. An'tia was the unicorn, right? Was he making fun of me? I rubbed my forehead. A slight headache was starting to pound behind my temples.

"Do you have any water?" I asked, ignoring his strange answer for now.

"Of course."

He turned to the wall to my left. "Andromeda, one hydrogen-oxygen fluid, please."

A hole appeared in the previously flawless white wall and a floating tumbler appeared in the gap. I stared at it, not believing my eyes. I had to be dreaming still. A dream within a dream.

Bruin took the container and the wall became solid

once more. If he wasn't holding a glass of water in his hand, I would have thought I'd imagined it all. Or maybe I was.

I pinched my arm. Ouch.

"What are you doing?" Bruin asked, aghast, staring at me with worry. "Why are you hurting yourself?"

"To see if I'm dreaming."

"You are not." He handed me the tumbler. It was made from heavy but paper-thin plastic. I sniffed the liquid. It didn't smell like anything, but I wasn't sure if that was reassuring or not.

I pushed myself up into a sitting position. Bruin looked like he wanted to help, but I was glad he didn't attempt to. The room swam before my eyes and I quickly focused on the tumbler in my hand. I took a small sip, relieved when it tasted like water should, like nothing.

"It is the same $H_2O$ you have on Peritus," Bruin said. "I made sure the formula has been programmed into the system."

Again, his words made no sense.

"Peritus?"

"Earth. Your planet."

"*Your* planet?" I parroted. "Mine, not yours?"

"Please look at the viewscreen. It will make things clearer."

He pointed at the window on the other side of the room. My vision was clearing, revealing a hexagonal room, empty except for a small round table in the centre, the bed I was lying on and a bench to my right.

No, I wasn't on a bed, I was on a second bench. Two identical doors on opposite walls and between them the window I'd refused to look at because what lay beyond couldn't be real...

"Very funny," I said without taking my eyes off the spacescape. It wasn't a window; in fact, Bruin had even called it a *viewscreen*. That made a lot more sense than thinking that we were in space. I must have bumped my head when fainting. I shouldn't have even considered that option.

"I am not called that very often. Attractive, charming, talented, yes. Funny, not so much. But I am pleased you find me amusing."

I tore my gaze away from the screen to look at Bruin. He was smiling, which softened the sharp features of his angular face. He was right. He was most definitely attractive. Not that it mattered right now.

"Where am I?" I demanded.

"On the Xylope, my ship. Well, the IGU's ship, but it's mine for this mission. You are an alien and I have abducted you."

His smile didn't waver. He seemed pleased with himself, until his eyebrows shot up and he fumbled with the strange wristwatch he wore. "Klat, that was the wrong way round. From your perspective, I'm the alien. Apologies. This is my first abduction."

"Abduction?" I echoed, my voice shrill. "You've abducted me?"

"It is permitted for scientific purposes as well as for star-bound mates. I have not done anything illegal."

I gaped at him. "You can't be serious. This is a joke, a prank. Did Sharon put you up to this? Or Tim?"

"I know neither a Sharon nor a Tim," he said calmly. "Technically, my sire instructed me to come to your planet, but it was I who chose to abduct you rather than one of the other natives. You are my – no, let's leave that for later. The manual said not to overwhelm you. Are you feeling overwhelmed?"

I opened my mouth, then closed it again. I had no words. Was I overwhelmed? Most definitely. Incredulous, angry, frustrated. I felt like I was at the butt end of a joke, yet nobody bothered to tell me the punch line.

"I forgot to inform you that I don't plan to eat you. Does that make it better?" Bruin looked mighty pleased with himself. I was starting to think he was crazy. I should have known. He'd been too perfect. Good-looking guys always turned out to be either in a relationship, crazy, arrogant dicks or idiots.

I glared at him, gathering all my anger and turning it into confidence. "Let me go or I will call the police."

"Police? Is that another one of your strange Peritan acronyms?"

He had to be pretending, yet I didn't spot a lie and I was good at reading people.

"Law enforcement. Clearer now?"

"Ah, yes, I understand. There's no need for that. You're safe with me."

He smiled again, as if that would make everything better.

"You must be fucking kidding me," I hissed. The time for politeness was over. This guy had kidnapped me. Probably. "You say you've abducted me, but I'm safe? Do you see that that's a big fat oxymoron?"

"I can see why it might seem that way, but trust me-"

"Trust you?! Do the people you abduct usually trust you? No, don't answer that. I'm leaving."

I stumbled to my feet, fighting a bout of dizziness. He didn't stop me. In fact, he stepped aside to open the way to the door. I somehow made it to the other end of the room, swaying as if drunk. The door slid open without a sound. A windowless corridor led to another door, but this one didn't open.

"Andromeda, give bridge access to Tara," I heard Bruin say from behind me.

As soon as he'd spoken, the door slid upwards into the ceiling, revealing a circular room with a glass dome roof. No, not glass, screens again, showing Earth and the darkness of space all around. In the centre sat a large chair that wouldn't have looked out of place on the set of Star Trek. Several smaller workstations were arranged in a circle around the central chair, but none were occupied.

"Do you believe me now?" Bruin asked softly, following me into the room.

"I had to admit, it's a very elaborate and expensive hoax, but no way are we really in space."

He looked a little disappointed, but then grinned.

"I know how to prove it. Andromeda, disengage artificial gravity on the bridge."

The strangest ever feeling took hold of my body, like floating in water without getting wet. And I was floating, actually floating! My feet hovered above the ground and even my arms were no longer pulled towards the floor. I'd never realised just how much I relied on gravity to stay upright. With it gone, I was a ship with neither anchor nor rudder.

"And now?" Bruin asked, grinning triumphantly. He looked a lot more at home in zero gravity, elegantly manoeuvring himself until he hovered above the centre chair.

I looked up at the dome – except that up was no longer up, it could have been any direction. The lack of gravity was making me more scared than Bruin's revelation of having abducted me had.

"Could you turn it back on?" I asked, hating to sound weak.

"Of course. Be ready, you'll feel very heavy in a click. Andromeda, engage artificial gravity."

He hadn't been lying. I was sucked towards the floor and almost fell to my knees. Bruin, on the other hand, landed elegantly in his chair. Bastard.

"It's time to say goodbye to Peritus," he said and waved cheerfully at the planet above us. My planet. Earth.

"Goodbye?" I croaked. "We're really in space?"

"We are."

"And... you're an alien?" I felt silly even voicing that question. This wasn't a film or a book, this was reality. Stuff like this didn't happen. Normal people didn't meet aliens.

"I am," he confirmed. "In a way, we're both aliens to one another. But since we're still in orbit of your planet, I suppose I'm more of an alien than you are."

"But you don't look like an alien. You look human."

"That's because I'm wearing a C-shield," he said, patting his wristwatch. "It tricks your eyes into seeing me as one of your own kind. Do you want me to turn it off?"

I nodded.

Without taking his eyes off me, he pressed his watch. The air around him shimmered and sparkled, before he turned purple.

Bruin was bright purple. His physical shape barely changed, he got even more muscular around the chest and arms, and his skull lengthened slightly. Way more noticeable was that his hair had disappeared. He was now completely bald, even his eyebrows were gone. He looked at me with a worried frown, as if he was concerned about what I might think now that I could see him for who he really was. I stared into his eyes, the same dark eyes that had captivated me back at the castle. There was no sign of menace or deceit. He was still the same.

"You're an alien," I whispered. "I've been abducted by an alien."

# LESSON 5

# RESEARCH FOR RENEGADES

## LESSON 5: RESEARCH FOR RENEGADES

BRUIN

I wasn't sure how I'd expected her to react. In my five days on Peritus, I'd noticed a lot of humans had prejudice against those with a different skin colour. Of course, my mate wasn't one of them, but I wouldn't have been surprised if she'd been a bit shocked at my change. After a cursory glance over my body, she'd looked me in the eyes, nodded to herself, then stared back at the observatory above us.

"I was kind of expecting several arms, tentacles and horns," she said. Her tense tone betrayed her easy-going words, but I didn't comment on it. She was handling it all remarkably well. I'd not planned to reveal myself this quickly, but there was no way I could refuse her wish. She was my mate. I was made to protect and serve her.

"On my planet, Allopo, there are three intelligent species, all quite similar at first glance but different nonetheless. Fervens have horns and are generally known to be quite aggressive and territorial. Bervens also have horns, but they grow wide rather than tall, and they're physically incapable of lying, making them favoured diplomats across the galaxy. And then there are us Xervens, without horns, but we make up with other features. Increased intelligence, for once. Our brains are bigger. And..."

I decided not to tell her about my dual cocks. I couldn't remember if Peritan males had one or several dicks, so it might not be all that special to Tara.

"And?" she asked.

"We're taller," I said quickly. Not a lie. The difference wasn't big, but in a crowd on Allopo, Xervens usually stood out.

"Wow. Is it normal for there to be three sentient species on the same planet? I guess on Earth we had the Neanderthals, but not anymore..." As her voice trailed off, she suddenly straightened and her curious gaze became a glare. "Don't bother. I don't care. You might think you have the right to abduct me just because you're an alien, but you don't. I demand that you return me to my home."

"Actually, I do have the right-"

That was the wrong thing to say. She screamed and launched herself at me. With no time to wonder where that sudden aggression had suddenly come from, I protectively crossed my arms in front of my face.

But she didn't aim at my face. She aimed at my crotch.

I winced when her fist crashed into my sacred rods. My knees felt weak as pain similar to being gored by a stabhorn ripped through me. I grit my teeth, unwilling to give her the satisfaction of hearing me scream. But Tara had already swirled around and run out of the room. I let her run. There was nowhere for her to go. She wouldn't know how to use the shuttle, nor had she the necessary clearance. She could explore the Xylope to her heart's content, but that was all she could do. There was no way back to the planet.

Perhaps it was better to remove the temptation. I set course for Allopo, letting the autopilot chart the best route. The Xylope was fully automated and had no need for a crew. The bridge was outfitted to accommodate a small team, but that was just for emergencies.

The journey would take twenty-two IG days, which was just over two IG weeks. Days on Allopo were slightly shorter, more like Peritan days, but since I spent most days with intergalactic visitors and colleagues, I was used to calculating in IG units. Something my sire had ingrained in me from the very beginning, back when he'd still hoped I'd follow in his footsteps and work for the IGU.

I pulled up a surveillance feed and asked Andromeda to search for Tara. My mate had made it to the cargo bay, where An'tia was waiting impatiently for her dinner. I hadn't even brushed her after beaming back onto the Xylope. I hoped she'd forgive me. An'tia was as arrogant as stabhorns came and very particular about her beauty routine. A day without at least two brushing sessions was a wasted day for her. I smiled when I realised just how much she'd wrapped me around her hooves already. And now Tara would soon do the same. I'd have two demanding females in my life, yet I didn't mind.

A new transmission was announced by a beep. I wasn't surprised to se my sire's name flick across the screen. The IGU had installed their own satellites around Peritus a few years ago, making real-time communication possible. I was tempted to reject his call, but then I'd just sit here and watch my mate like a stalker. Maybe this was just the distraction I needed.

With a sigh, I took the call and waited until my sire appeared as a hologram in front of me. His stern gaze triggered familiar feelings of inadequacy.

"Have you succeeded in your abduction yet? I have received your preliminary research reports. I'm surprised by their quality."

I wanted to roll my eyes like Peritans did, but I was physically unable to. Of course, he was surprised by my abilities. He'd never taken the time to focus on what I *could* do, instead always highlighting my many faults and failures.

"I have successfully abducted a female," I replied, keeping my voice neutral. "She's acclimatising to her new surroundings just now. I found the IGU guide very helpful."

I added the last bit to appeal to my sire's pride. It might distract him from asking questions about how I'd chosen the female.

"Good," he said. "Once she's accepted her situation, you can begin to study her interactions with the stabhorn. Why did you only abduct the one specimen?"

Internally, I cringed at his choice of words, but I knew him well enough to know that he was goading me.

"The stabhorn reacted positively towards her. I thought that would be an interesting aspect to study further, and adding more research subjects might spoil the results."

My sire looked at me with something like appreciation. Not pride, never, but it wasn't the disappointment I usually had to endure. "I agree, that is an unusual and fascinating behaviour. For now, study the Peritan as closely as possible. Record every interaction between her and the stabhorn. In the meantime, I will continue going over your existing reports and put together a list of what needs to be improved. Your style isn't academic enough, but if I have the time, I will rewrite some of them to give you an example of how they should be done in future."

I didn't tell him that there would be no future. I was doing this to pay off my debts, not to become a permanent researcher at the IGU. Once my mate had got used to living on Allopo, I'd go back to being a stabhorn tamer. Minus the groupies. From now on, no other female would ever get to see, taste or feel my cock again. Only my mate. The days of playing around were over.

"Based on your experiences on Peritus," my sire continued, "do you agree with my hypothesis that a kind of stabhorn was once present on the planet, but has since become extinct? It would be the perfect explanation for the stabhorns in their mythology."

"Maybe," I hedged. "Wouldn't there be fossil records if that was true?"

"Not necessarily. And we'd have to trust their archaeologists to find all the right fossils. They're lacking the experience and technology to build a complete fossil record."

"Then you might be right. I saw stabhorns in all sorts of places on Peritus, even on crockery and in younglings' books. They're everywhere. And in one country, Scotland, their version of the stabhorn is recognised as a national animal."

"I know, fascinating." My sire smiled, enthusiasm softening his stern features. I burned the image into my memory. My sire, smiling. That happened once every few rotations at most. Something to tell the grand-younglings.

"I better go. I don't want to leave my abductee alone for too long," I said and ended the call. Pulling up the surveillance screen again, I watched with amusement as Tara was gently brushing An'tia. That devious stabhorn had already found a new servant. I didn't know how she'd done it, but I'd find out once I watched the recordings later. For now, I wanted to be back with my mate. I'd given her some time. Ten IG minutes should be enough to calm down, right?

# LESSON 6

# UNICORN CARE 101

## LESSON 6: UNICORN CARE 101

TARA

The spaceship wasn't as big as I'd expected. I found several unused bedrooms, some with bunk beds like on an actual ship, until I walked down some steps and into a large hangar. I assumed this would be used for storage, but right now, it was almost empty. The only occupant was the unicorn, lying on a huge red rug in the centre of the hangar. An empty trough stood on one side, while an assortment of brushes and other instruments was laid out on a small table. For a second, I wondered where the unicorn went to the toilet, then quickly pushed that thought from my mind. Unicorns were magical and I didn't want to spoil that by thinking about practicalities.

An'tia whinnied softly when I approached. Now that I knew she was an actual unicorn and not just a horse with a stuck-on horn, I had even more respect for her.

"Did he abduct you, too?" I asked and looked up into her big, turquoise eyes. Then I remembered how I'd been sucked in the last time and quickly focused on her mane. "Or did you come willingly? And are you an actual unicorn or just an alien animal that coincidentally looks like one?"

An'tia didn't respond. Not that I'd expected her to. But for some strange reason, I thought she understood what I was saying.

With a snort, she picked up one of the brushes with her perfectly white teeth and held it out to me.

"You want me to brush you?"

She snorted again, as if to say, 'obviously'.

I was still intimidated by her size - and by her being an alien animal, not just a bog-standard horse - but I didn't feel like she meant me any harm. I'd just have to stay clear of her hooves and her tail. And her horn, obviously.

I took the brush and held it out in front of me, letting An'tia decide where she wanted to be groomed. She pressed her neck against the brush, so I started with her mane. The hair was silky smooth and the brush glid over it easily.

"I wish my hair was as soft as yours," I muttered. "If you were human, I'd ask what kind of product you use. Does Bruin groom you every day? Does he wash your mane or is that unnecessary?"

An'tia huffed impatiently. I clearly wasn't working

fast enough for her. I was too small to reach the top of her head, but she lowered herself onto her knees before I could even ask. Clever unicorn. When I brushed her between her ears, she whinnied happily.

"You like that, huh? Do you want me to keep the ribbons in or remove them?"

"Keep them," a voice said from behind me.

I whirled around, holding the brush like a weapon. Bruin had entered the hangar without me noticing. He slowly held up his hands, as if motioning to a frightened animal.

"I come in peace. Thanks for grooming An'tia. I haven't had time yet for her second brushing session."

"Second?"

"Aye, I already groomed her for over an IG hour this morning before we continued our search for you."

He stopped, an uncomfortable expression replacing his easy smile. He'd said something he'd not intended to voice.

"Search for me? *Me* specifically?" The anger that had only just abated returned with full force. "You didn't just abduct me, you also stalked me?!"

"It's not like that," he started, but I cut him off.

"I don't know what I'm even doing here. Grooming a unicorn while I should be trying to get home. Are you going to bring me back to Earth?"

An'tia nudged the small of my back, but I ignored her. I didn't want to lose my fury again. Her peaceful presence had made me forget for just a moment that I was a captive here. That I'd been taken against my will. I wouldn't let her distract me from my righteous anger.

"No," he said softly. Was that regret swinging in his melodic voice, or did I imagine that? "I'm sorry. I can't."

The bastard actually looked apologetic, which only made me angrier.

"Why not?" I snarled. Anger was burning in my veins and I felt like hitting something. Or someone, if a certain alien got in my way.

"Because I can't. You are... I need you."

"Need me? For some experiment? Are you going to probe me?!" I sounded hysterical, but I didn't care. I had a right to be furious.

"Nothing like that," he said, still calm as a purple cucumber. "I have to study how you react to An'tia and if you start believing in her existence."

I turned to look at the unicorn, then back at Bruin. Confusion warred with anger. "Are you saying An'tia isn't real? Am I hallucinating? Oh fuck, are we not in space at all? Is this some kind of drug-induced trip?"

"No, you got it all wrong." Bruin sounded just as confused as I felt. "She's real, as real as you and I. If I promise to explain everything, will you calm down?"

"I will calm down if you promise to take me home," I snapped.

"I can't make that promise. But you might change your mind once you know the truth. Calm down, please?"

His soulful dark eyes were begging me to listen to him. Fuck that man. I couldn't just give in. Although would it really hurt to postpone my next angry outburst and find out what was really going on?

"You have five minutes," I said coldly.

"Do you mind if I join you in grooming An'tia? Her horn needs polishing."

I was very tempted to say no, but I also didn't want to go anywhere near the unicorn's sharp horn.

"Go ahead, but don't you dare touch me."

He smiled and took a cloth from the table. I kept some safe distance between us and started brushing An'tia's hind quarters. Grooming her gave me something to focus on that wasn't related to Bruin.

He stayed silent for a minute while he gently ran the cloth over her horn. An'tia seemed to enjoy it. Could a unicorn like someone who was evil? All the legends said that they were attracted to innocent virgins, but it was possible the myths got it wrong. Maybe space unicorns liked rogues and rebels instead of virgins.

"My sire is a professor at the Intergalactic University," Bruin began slowly. He didn't look at me, instead preferring to focus on An'tia. "He researches Peritans - humans, that is. I am a stabhorn tamer. A rather successful one, actually. Not long ago-"

"Stabhorn?" I interrupted. "Is that what you call An'tia?"

"Yes, she's a venom-tipped stabhorn, very rare. And she almost killed me. Stabbed me in the belly. The wound on its own wouldn't have been fatal, but in combination with the poison... let's just say I'm lucky to be alive."

I was tempted to step away from An'tia, now that she'd been revealed as a deadly animal, but that would have been admitting fear. I didn't want Bruin to think me weak.

"My medical treatment was expensive," he continued. "It got me into debt. Big debt. I would have lost everything, but then my sire offered me a way out. He read about the animals you call unicorns in your Peritan literature and was intrigued. Since I know all about stabhorns, he sent An'tia and me to Peritus. Our mission is to study Peritans' reaction to her and whether they believe that she's a unicorn or not. My sire thinks that will lead to other critical conclusions about Peritan behaviour and thought processes. While we travelled your world, I took notes and did some recordings that my sire can analyse. But he also asked me to abduct one or more Peritans to do a more in-depth study with."

"Me," I gasped. "You said you weren't going to probe me."

"I have no intentions of probing you. Unless you so desire." He gave me a cheeky grin that caused a totally inappropriate flutter in my belly. "I have heard it can be very pleasurable."

I ignored that comment. "So your father wants to see how I react to An'tia. Well, here I am, brushing her. Is that enough? Can I go home now?"

"No. He will want a lot more data. I will have to

monitor your vitals while you interact with An'tia. He's also given me a list of questions to ask you. And he might have other tests for you once we arrive on Allopo."

"What happens after? Once you've done all your tests? Will you return me to Earth?"

"No." His refusal was absolute.

"Why not?"

He finally met my gaze. His eyes were smouldering flecks of coal. "Because you're my mate."

# LESSON 7

# HYSTERIA FOR HUMANS

## LESSON 7: HYSTERIA FOR HUMANS

BRUIN

I wasn't sure what I'd expected her reaction to be. Not quite an instant declaration of love, but maybe pleasant surprise. A moment of shock, then overwhelming happiness. Instead, she started laughing. She threw her head back, her hair rippling like a golden wave, and laughed. It was a strangled sort of laugh, too high and without any humour.

I stared at her, not knowing what to do. Was this normal Peritan behaviour? Did laughter mean something else in their culture? No, I would have noticed that on the five days I'd spent travelling their planet. Laughter was almost universal across the galaxy. With a few rare exceptions, every species had a sense of humour. Granted, sometimes it varied so vastly from that of another species that wars had been fought over misunderstood jokes, but in general, you could assume that every alien you came across either could laugh or at least understood the concept.

Tara didn't stop. When she started wheezing and gasping for breath, I took a step towards her. If she needed medical attention, I wanted to be close. Maybe I should get her into the medpod. All this laughter couldn't be good for her. Tara's cheeks had become bright red. The colour suited her, although I would have preferred purple over red.

"What's wrong?" I asked cautiously. "Why are you laughing?"

She wiped fluid from her eyes. "Just... this isn't happening."

Another giggle broke from her throat.

I was starting to get really worried. "How do I make it stop?"

She made a choking sound. That was the signal to get her the medical care she clearly needed. Ignoring her protest, I bundled her into my arms and raced to the medpod at the other end of the hangar. A feeling of cold dread was spreading through my innards. My mate wasn't well and it was all my fault.

"What are you... hick... doing? Let me... hick... go!"

Now she couldn't even speak properly. Something was seriously wrong with her. She struggled against my hold, but I was stronger. I pressed her arms against her sides so that she wouldn't hurt herself. She was too weak to do much against it, which only worried me further. My mate was so defenceless. How did her species survive? Xervens didn't have the horns of the other two sentient species on my planet, but we were bigger and more intelligent, adding to our chances of survival. In my opinion, we were the dominant species on Allopo, but of course, Fervens and Bervens would disagree.

"Stop struggling. I'm only trying to help you," I told her as calmly as I could.

The medpod slid open when we approached and I lowered her into the gel.

"Ewwww... hick... that's disgusting!" she exclaimed, followed by another bout of laughter.

I closed the lid above her and ordered the pod to run a full diagnostic sequence once for the second time today. I waited impatiently as the data rolled over the screen. Her oxygen levels were low, but the pod had already automatically flooded with the gas to help return them to normal. All the other values were fine. Physically, my mate was healthy, but that didn't reassure me. What if I'd broken her mind? Telling her that she was my mate had been a bad decision. She'd only just discovered that I was an alien and that unicorns were real. I'd forgotten how sheltered Peritans were. And now it was my fault if I'd fractured her mind forever.

For a fraction of a click, I considered returning her to her planet. But no, now that we'd met the mating bond would make any separation painful for both of us. I could live with pain, but not with the knowledge that my mate was suffering. She had to stay by my side. Once we'd completed the starlight ritual, we'd be able to be apart once more, although it would never feel comfortable. At least that's what I'd been told. The soulmate bond was rare and therefore almost mystical. Not many people found their soulmates. Many more never found theirs, while others spent half their lives searching. It was a miracle that I had found mine on the planet I just happened to be visiting. Maybe this was fate making up for me almost dying.

As soon as the medpod had returned Tara's oxygen levels to normal, the lid opened with a hiss. She climbed out and crossed her arms in front of her chest, glaring at me. But at least her laughter had stopped.

"How are you feeling?" I asked cautiously.

She didn't reply, but her glare seemed to get even more intense. If she'd been a Kravuton rather than a harmless Peritan, I would have expected fire to burst from her mouth and nostrils. Although not quite harmless. She'd already ripped a hole in my heart. Time would tell if she would heal or break it.

"Are you hungry?" I tried, realising I'd not fed her since arriving on the Xylope. How often did Peritans need to be fed and watered? I would have to check the guide. Something told me that my mate would not be happy if she didn't get food at regular intervals.

"No."

She spat out the word. It hurt to see her this cold.

"Do you want to sleep?"

"No."

"Do you want to groom An'tia some more?"

"No."

I hated myself for forcing her to stay with me. If only she could see that it was for her own good. Would it help if I told her? Probably not, but it was worth a try.

"If I take you home now, you'd be in pain. You are my soulmate and touching you has started the bonding process. It will have to be completed, or we will both suffer the consequences."

She didn't respond.

"Soulmates are special," I tried again. "It's very rare. It means we're destined to be together by fate itself. You are the most perfect mate for me in the entire universe. And the other way round, although it would be arrogant to suggest that I am perfect."

"It would be," she muttered.

"I know this will all seem very strange to you, but I promise, once we get to know each other, you will see that we are meant to be. The stars have brought us together for a reason."

"Let me guess, to have lots and lots of babies?" Her voice was emotionless. It hurt to hear her talk like that.

"We can have younglings, and I would very much wish to be a sire one day, but only if you want to. I know you don't think much of me just now, but I will never force you to do anything you don't want to do. I am sorry I can't take you home, but as I said, it would hurt. The bond will keep driving us together by force. I've heard it's unpleasant to try and go against it."

"So I don't have a choice? How is that not forced? It might not be you, but this supposed bond is just as bad.

I don't want to be mated to you. I don't want to be your soulmate."

Her words cut deeper than any blade ever could. She was rejecting me. She didn't know that it was possible to reject a soulmate bond, but it took a great deal of strength. I doubted she'd be strong enough. She wouldn't survive the process, so I kept quiet and didn't tell her about it. I'd rather she hate me than risk her life.

"I have dreamed of you," I said instead, surprising myself. Suddenly it all made sense. "When I was close to death, I dreamed of you. Your golden hair. Your voice. I heard you in my dream, although I couldn't understand what you were saying. I didn't remember until now, but my memory is crystal clear all of a sudden. You held me. Protected me. Maybe you even stopped me from floating into the Eternal River of Souls to join my ancestors."

"In any other situation, I'd say that's almost romantic," she scoffed. "But it doesn't change anything."

Still, her voice wasn't quite as cold anymore. Her glare had lessened in intensity, going from scorching to a flickering flame.

She needed time. Time to process, time to come to understand that we were made for each other. She'd get to know me and realise that I was a good person. And then, we could conduct the starlight ritual and cement our mating bond.

"I will show you your room," I said, forcing myself to turn away from her. "And then I will bring you some Xerven delicacies. You must be hungry by now."

She didn't move to follow me. "Are you going to lock me up?"

I stopped in my tracks, aghast. "Of course not! You are free to move around the Xylope as much as you want. I just thought you might want some time to yourself. Sleep a little. Get some rest."

"That's...thoughtful of you."

I counted that as a victory. When I started walking again, she followed. I led her to one of the empty bedrooms, two doors down from my own. As much as I wanted her close to me, I realised she needed space. She didn't need to know that I'd keep an eye on her to make sure she was alright. The laughing thing had scared me. I would not lose my mate, no matter what I'd have to do.

# LESSON 8
# SULKING
# STUDIES

# LESSON 8: SULKING STUDIES

TARA

I avoided him for the next three days, ghosting through the spaceship, hurrying in the opposite direction every time I heard him approach. Every few hours, a meal would automatically appear on the table in my little room. The AI learned what I liked with every dish and repeated only the ones I'd enjoyed. All of the meals were alien and I never quite knew what I was eating. Sometimes I wasn't even sure if it was meat or vegetables.

My room was small, with every inch of space used efficiently. The bed disappeared into the wall every morning and instead, a table and a comfy chair rose from the floor. I never figured out how that technology worked. When the bed was there, the floor was seamless, yet the other furniture had to come from somewhere. In one corner, a toilet magically grew out of the wall whenever I told the ship that I needed the loo. It had taken me a way to get used to peeing in a plastic beaker attached to a pipe that started to suck as soon as I held it to... certain body parts. I supposed it would also work if we lost the artificial gravity, but it was still weird. Instead of washing my hands in a sink, I pressed them on a blue spot on the wall and turquoise mist would envelop them, leaving my skin refreshed and smelling of violets. Still, I didn't like that my bedroom was also my bathroom. Efficient, yes, but not how I wanted to live long-term. I would have liked to ask Bruin how long we'd travel on the Xylope, but that would have meant talking to him. No, thanks. I preferred to be on my own.

Another thing I didn't like was that the bed didn't have a duvet or even a blanket. The mattress was warm, the perfect temperature actually, but I missed having something to wrap around me for comfort. I slept in my tour guide uniform the first night, but when I woke up in the morning - or at least I assumed it was morning, it was hard to tell without daylight - a stack of clothes was waiting for me on the end of my bed. I wasn't sure if Bruin or the ship's AI had provided them. After finding some very lacy lingerie among the stack, I hoped it was the AI.

After three days, I started to smell, so I asked the ship to show me to a shower. Light strips appeared on the floor, guiding me to a door at the end of the corridor. I could swear it hadn't existed before. I'd explored the entire ship and snooped into every room.

This one was completely empty save for three narrow shelves attached to one wall. No, they were part of the wall and I bet they could be sucked in like the other furniture. The door slid closed behind me. The ceiling glowed dimly, making it feel like a cosy cave.

Assuming that water would somehow spurt from the ceiling without the need for a shower head or faucet, I took off my clothes and placed them on the shelves. I stood in the centre of the room and waited, but nothing happened. Stretching out my arms, I waved, just in case there was a motion sensor. Nothing.

"Andromeda, start the shower."

Still no water. I was about to get dressed again when a thick white fog streamed from unseen holes in the walls, covering the floor in an instant. When it reached my feet, I jumped, surprised by how warm and wet the fog felt. That had to be the alternative to a shower – unless Bruin had programmed the room to suffocate me. Unlikely. Despite everything, I'd come to believe that his heart was in the right place. If he even had a heart. I shouldn't assume that his anatomy matched mine.

The fog rose quickly, but stopped when it wavered around my shoulders. I rubbed my hands over my skin, although that was probably unnecessary. I squeezed my eyes shut and bent down to get my hair fully immersed in the warm fog. My hair turned wet instantly, sticking to my skin. I ran a hand through it. So smooth. The fog had no scent, but there had to be some kind of soap contained within.

After a minute or two, just when I wondered what I was supposed to do next, the fog slowly dissipated. For a fraction of a second, the air turned hot, but then the temperature returned to normal. My hair no longer felt as heavy. I held up a strand. Dry and shiny. Perfect. Fastest hair dryer ever. I could get used to that.

In the following days, I had a shower every morning, then went to say hello to An'tia. The unicorn got less intimidating with each visit. I even polished her horn when she begged for it. She pointed at whatever brush or cloth she wanted me to use, then left me to figure out where she liked it the most. I quickly discovered her favourite spot to scratch was between her ears and along her belly.

And still, I avoided Bruin. I assumed he was keeping an eye on me electronically, even though I'd been unable to spot any cameras. He gave me the space I needed, but at the same time, I felt like this was only the calm before the storm. Eventually, I'd have to talk to him again. And find a way to persuade him that I had to return to Earth.

After about a week, I decided that I'd sulked long enough. I needed to face my fears – or in this case, Bruin.

I FOUND him on the bridge, lost in thought. He didn't notice me enter. The darkness of space loomed outside. I'd avoided looking at space until now. I didn't want to be reminded how far from home I was. Besides, the emptiness outside the ship was frightening. I couldn't wrap my mind around how we were floating through empty space, the only lifeforms in this part of the universe.

"What's the nearest planet?" I asked, startling Bruin.

He jumped off his chair and swirled around to face me. "VX9821, but it's an uninhabited gas giant. The closest inhabited planet is Quendrin, about two lightyears away. It's on the Galactic Council's banned list of planets, however, so it cannot be visited until the local sentient species is more evolved." He gave me a cautious smile, as if worried how I'd react. "Your planet was on the same list until recently. Even now, only research ships are allowed to breach the atmosphere."

I swallowed a harsh remark that even research ships shouldn't be allowed to abduct humans. I'd come here intending to stay civil and get some answers. A week's worth of questions was waiting to be asked.

I flopped down in one of the smaller chairs. Bruin visibly relaxed when he saw that I wasn't going to scream at him again.

"How are you feeling?" he asked after a while. "Any more strange laughing episodes?"

"You would have seen them."

He didn't deny it, confirming that he'd indeed been watching me.

I sighed. "Well, besides being abducted from my home, I'm okay. But how do you do it?"

"Do what?"

I pointed at the dome above us. "Look at space. It's so...lonely."

"The first time I left my planet, I found it frightening, too," he admitted. "My sire didn't understand. He told me to suck it up and be strong. So I pretended to be alright with it, but inside, I continued to be scared."

"When did it change?"

He looked me right in the eyes. "The moment you joined me on board the Xylope. Until then, I'd felt alone every time I travelled through space. Even when surrounded by other travellers or my sire, the loneliness didn't go away. I think it's the absence of light out there. It feels like you're the only person in-"

"All of space," I finished the sentence for him.

"Exactly. But with you, it's different. Now I can look out into space and enjoy the view. I know I'm no longer alone."

His words both touched me and made me uncomfortable at the same time. He didn't even know me. We were strangers, no matter what he'd said about soulmates.

Bruin sat down again and we stayed quiet for a while. It was a comfortable silence as we both looked at the stars sparkling in the darkness. Tiny spots of hope in a sea of despair. That's how they'd seemed to me yesterday. And now? I wasn't so sure anymore.

"How much further is it to your planet?" I asked eventually.

"Sixteen IG days. That's eighteen Peritan days, if I'm not mistaken."

"How long is an IG day?"

"Twenty-seven of your hours. You're one of the lucky planets where the difference isn't all that big. The conversion is a lot more complicated for other alien species."

He did something with his wristwatch and a star map appeared on one of the screens. A dot flickered in a particularly empty spot.

"That's us," Bruin explained. "And this is our route."

A dashed line materialised on the map.

"Why isn't it a straight line?" I asked. "This doesn't look like the fastest route."

"There are planets in the way. Because of their gravitational fields, we have to circle around them. And there will be asteroid fields, space debris and other obstacles. The AI has selected the best route for us and it's rarely wrong."

"Rarely?"

"Never."

"Then why did you say rarely?"

He shot me a sheepish look. "My sire's bad influence. He believes there's an exception to everything. And he sees me as living proof for that."

His smile disappeared as a shadow crossed his face.

"Why?" I asked.

"I suppose you need to know. I was not born in the conventional way. My sire doesn't have a mate, but he desired to have an heir, so he had me created. I'm his clone."

It took a few seconds for his words to sink in. A clone. He didn't have a mother. Instead of shock, all I felt for him was pity.

"I'm sorry," I said and meant it. "It can't have been easy to grow up without a mum."

He looked at me in surprise. "You're not repulsed? Do you understand what I am? I was created in a lab. It has become more commonplace now, but it's still not fully accepted on Allopo. There are some Ferven cultists who believe clones don't have a soul."

"Do you think you have one?"

Bruin didn't hesitate. "Yes. Sometimes I think I have more of a soul than my sire. He's a brilliant male when it comes to his work, but he wasn't a good sire. Nor is he particularly nice to his colleagues. Come to think of it, I doubt there's anyone he likes."

"He doesn't sound very pleasant," I said.

"He isn't. I hope you won't think badly of me when you meet him. I might be his clone, but I'm nothing like my sire. It's why he thinks I'm a failed clone. I should be his identical copy, but somewhere along the line, I got my own personality. I look like him, though."

I supposed seeing his father would be like looking into Bruin's future. How did Xervens age? He didn't have any hair that could go grey and I couldn't imagine wrinkles or liver spots on his smooth purple skin.

"Speaking of my father," Bruin continued, "I need to ask you the questions he sent me. He's been reminding me every day, but I wanted to give you some time."

I was grateful, even though that didn't mean I'd forgiven him for abducting me. Nor had I given up on finding a way home. For now, it was no use fighting Bruin. He'd made it clear that he wouldn't change the ship's course. But maybe once he realised that we weren't actually mates, he'd let me go. And if he didn't realise that on his own, I'd have to force him.

# LESSON 9

# FIRST
# ASSESSMENT

## LESSON 9: FIRST ASSESSMENT

BRUIN

I t had taken her longer than expected to come to her senses. I'd kept a constant eye on her, fascinated by how she explored the ship and interacted with An'tia. The situation would have been a lot worse without the stabhorn. She was the intermediary between the two of us. An'tia connected us even though we'd not been in the same room for the entire week.

Whenever Tara had left the stabhorn to do other things, I'd taken her place. Because of that, An'tia had turned into the most spoilt stabhorn in the universe. Two people to groom and dote on her. She took full advantage of it, demanding me to brush her even when I knew Tara had just done the same.

When I wasn't with An'tia, I worked on the reports for my sire. He'd sent me his notes on the preliminary observations and I'd made the requested changes. He'd demanded surprisingly few corrections. Maybe he'd finally realised that I wasn't as useless as he thought.

I'd written some notes on how Tara interacted with An'tia, but I wasn't ready to share those yet. I'd have to make sure there was no subtext that would suggest I was mated to the Peritan. He'd find out eventually, but I wanted to choose the right moment to tell him.

My plan had been to ask Tara tomorrow if she was ready to go through the questionnaire with me. I was glad she'd come to me instead. Maybe she'd finally accepted that I was her mate. I didn't want to talk about the topic yet, too worried that it might result in another medical emergency.

Realising I'd been quiet for a while, I pulled up the questions on my Commband's holo screen.

"I will record you, is that alright?" I asked.

"What will happen with the recording?"

"It will be automatically transcribed. My sire might take a look at it, but the IGU's data protection guidelines are among the strictest in the galaxy. The recording won't be shared with anyone else outside his research group."

"I guess that's alright then." She leaned back, reassuringly relaxed in my presence. "Shoot."

"What?"

Tara smiled. The entire room seemed to brighten. "Don't take that literally. It means I want you to start."

"Ah. Then I shall shoot." I returned her smile,

proud I was using a Peritanism. "Do you believe that An'tia is real?"

Her forehead wrinkled. "Of course."

"Do you believe that there are other animals like An'tia?"

"You said you tame stabhorns, so I have no reason to doubt that there are others."

I had a suspicion I'd tainted the results. My sire wouldn't be happy. I ignored it for now and continued with the questions.

"Back on Peritus, did you believe in stabhorns?"

Tara shook her head. "Neither in stabhorns nor in unicorns. Although I always told the tourists that I believed in unicorns since it's Scotland's national animal. They liked that."

"Do you know any Peritans who believe in stab...unicorns?"

"I don't think so. Some of the other tour guides pretended to, but I'm pretty sure it was a joke. Some children I led around the castle definitely believed in unicorns, but they also believed in Santa and the Easter bunny. There's something strange though that I've thought about a lot in the past few days. I once read this book, *The Unicorn Herd*. I can't remember the author's name, but now that I've met an actual unicorn, I have to admit it was strangely realistic. Do you think the author could have met an actual unicorn?"

"Tape, Arizona," I said and watched with amusement as her eyes widened in surprise. "I've read it as part of my research. Much more realistic than *Once*

*Upon a Unicorn*, in which the stabhorn is born without a horn. How preposterous. And don't get me started on *The Little Llama Meets a Unicorn*. The llama, which seems to be one of your Peritan land animals, actually becomes a stabhorn. Impossible."

"We sold *Once Upon a Unicorn* at the castle gift shop!" she exclaimed. "I can't believe we both read the same books even though you're an alien. What are the chances?"

"I am not surprised. You are my mate. It is only natural that we would have similar interests."

Her smile disappeared in an instant. Her eyes turned cold. "I am not your mate."

It hurt to hear her say that, but I didn't try to convince her otherwise. She'd realise the truth at some point. Until then, I had to be patient. It wasn't easy, with my mating cock swollen inside its sheath. I'd tried hard to distract myself from the urge to claim her with both my cocks, complete the starlight ritual, but it was getting more difficult with every day. Now I knew why some males went mad with mating lust.

I returned my attention to the questionnaire. Some of the questions were too silly to ask. My sire would just have to go without answers to those.

"Now that you've met An'tia, would you tell other Peritans about her? Would you try and convince them that unicorns are real?"

She thought for a moment. "As much as I'd want to, they wouldn't take me seriously. Nobody would believe me. They'd either assume I was joking or that I've gone crazy. So no, I don't think I would."

"Last question. Would you tell other Peritans if there was a group of you?"

"If we'd all met An'tia? Maybe. It's more likely, but even so, I still don't think we'd be taken seriously." Tara's smile returned. "Even if we brought proof with us, people would think it's fabricated. Fake news, they call it nowadays. Maybe it's better if nobody knows that stabhorns exist. I don't think humans are ready for them yet."

I grinned. "Nobody will ever be ready for stabhorns. And I say that as someone who was almost killed by one."

My left hand automatically wandered to my stomach. No scar remained, but I didn't need a physical mark to remember the trauma. At the same time, without that accident, I would never have met An'tia.

I gasped at the realisation.

"What is it?" Tara asked.

"An'tia didn't just find you on Peritus. She brought us together. I've been racking my brain about why she stabbed me. She was frightened, but not enough to charge me. I'm usually good with new arrivals. I have enough experience to know how far to push them. I might end up getting kicked or scratched with a horn, but not stabbed. I thought I was losing my touch, but that doesn't match how much An'tia trusts me now. In fact, she stopped rebelling almost as soon as we were on the ship to Peritus. She must have known that injuring me would set me on the path to your planet."

Tara didn't look convinced, but I was sure I'd figured it all out.

"How would she have known that your sire would offer you the job?" she asked.

"I don't know. But it's said that stabhorns have a unique connection to the universe. They know what will happen before it does. And, of course, they're able to find soulmates. It must be part of that magical skill."

"Magic?" she repeated, sounding even more doubtful.

"A token word for anything that cannot yet be explained by science." I stopped when I noticed I sounded like my sire. He would say that when I was still a youngling and believed in the fairy tales the nanny told me.

"It still seems far-fetched to me, but I'm not a stabhorn expert. Is there a way to ask her? I've been wondering how much she understands. How clever are stabhorns?"

"They are more intelligent than most people assume," I explained. "I have the suspicion that they purposely make us underestimate them. They're not just mere beasts. They have a societal structure, they have learned behaviour that gets passed down through generations, they have a sort of language."

"Language?" Tara gasped. "Does that mean you can talk to them?"

"No, so far, nobody has been able to add their

language to our translation implants. But if someone ever figures it out, I will add it to your implant immediately."

I realised too late that I'd never told her about the implant. Klat.

# LESSON 10

# REDEMPTION FOR REBELS

# LESSON 10: REDEMPTION FOR REBELS

TARA

Just when I'd started to trust him again, he had to destroy everything.

"Implant?" I snapped. "Are you saying you put an implant in me?!"

He had the decency to look guilty.

"I thought I'd mentioned it. When I first brought you on board, I gave you a full medical screening to make sure the beaming hadn't harmed you. It seemed a good opportunity to fit you with a translation implant and to remove the foreign body from your uterus."

Foreign body... he hadn't. Surely, he hadn't.

"You. Removed. My. IUD?!" I was screaming, but I didn't care. "How dare you!"

Bruin looked crestfallen. "IUD? Was it important? I thought it was harmful. I promise I wouldn't have removed it otherwise. Are you alright without it? Will you survive?"

Panic slurred his words.

In any other situation, I would have found it adorable, amusing even. But he'd removed my contraception without asking me. That went too far. I felt violated. I'd thought I was in control of my body, yet he'd shown me that I wasn't.

"Please, tell me," Bruin begged. "Are you in danger?"

No, but *he* was. I was about ready to murder him. Except that would have taken my moral high ground.

For a moment, I was tempted to let him believe I was dying. That would serve him right.

"An IUD is a contraceptive implant," I snapped. "It stops me from getting pregnant. I suppose you don't have things like that. You kidnap women and breed them until they can't pop out any more babies."

He stared at me in shock, but then fierce determination took over his features. "I would *never* do that," he said sternly. "And we do have contraception, just not this... primitive."

Primitive. I wanted to strangle him. Then push the implant up his dick. That should hurt. If he even had one. My gaze wandered to his crotch before I could stop myself. There was a bulge pressing against his black trousers, but that could have been anything. He was an alien, as he'd just proved once more.

"Put it back in," I demanded.

"Of course. I will see if the medpod can return your implant to where it was before. Alternatively, I can get you a Xerven implant. It is much smaller and won't hurt at all."

I didn't think I could trust that after all this.

"I want my implant. My coil. Sterilised, obviously."

"The medpod will ensure it's safe," Bruin reassured me, still looking incredibly guilty. "How can I make it up to you?"

"I don't suppose you'd take me home?"

His sad puppy eyes were answer enough.

THIS TIME, I went into the medpod voluntarily. The gel-like substance was warm, wrapping itself around me. I felt it permeate my clothes, but it wasn't the same sensation as wearing wet clothes. The gel was unlike anything I'd ever encountered. It likely had some fancy, complicated name.

When the lid closed above me, I fought a wave of claustrophobia. Bruin waved at me through the translucent lid.

"Try and stay still while the medpod attempts to reimplant your IDD."

"IUD," I muttered, but did as instructed. I did not want the coil to end up in my ovaries.

"All done," he said a minute later. "I triple-checked that it works. Copper release is a strange method of contraception, but if that's what you prefer, I fully support you. And if you ever want to switch to something more modern, it's quick and easy. Any medpod can do it."

The lid opened. Bruin stretched out a hand to help me out, but I ignored him and climbed out myself. The gel stayed behind, leaving my clothes spotless.

A loud whinny reminded me that the medpod was in An'tia's domain. The unicorn stood on the other side of the hangar, watching curiously. She wasn't quite interested enough to walk over – I'd quickly learned that An'tia was a lazy lady who didn't move unless she absolutely had to.

As soon as I reached her, she pointed her horn at the biggest brush on the table. I took it, but then reconsidered.

"Before I start, I need to ask you a question. Did you stab Bruin on purpose? To make him leave his planet? To find me?"

An'tia snorted and a cloud of golden dust exploded from her nostrils. Was that a yes? No?

I had to know.

"I think you understand me," I told her. "If you think Bruin and I are mates, pick up the cloth."

The stabhorn looked at me as if I was stupid, then turned to the table and lifted the polishing cloth with her teeth. Since that could have been a coincidence, I tried again.

"If you instigated all this, if you stabbed Bruin so that he would find me, kick the table."

She shot me an exasperated look before knocking over the table. Brushes and tools flew to the floor, while the stabhorn looked on with glee.

"Why haven't you communicated with me before?" I asked in wonder.

I bet she would have rolled her eyes if she could have. Because I hadn't asked the right questions. I'd treated her like a horse, assuming her intelligence matched an Earth animal. It was all on me.

The stipulations of what I'd just discovered sent shockwaves through my mind. Bruin really was my soulmate. I didn't believe it from his lips, but An'tia was different. She was a unicorn. I trusted her. She'd stabbed Bruin to get him to me, risked his death just to play matchmaker. If that was how far she went to instigate a meeting, I didn't know what she'd do to ensure we stayed together.

It was strange how my entire outlook had suddenly changed. I'd never believed in fate, but I did believe in unicorns now. If An'tia thought Bruin and I were supposed to be together, I was willing to try.

I turned to Bruin, who'd stayed a few steps behind, watching us. Hurrying over to him, I looked into his smouldering eyes. "Is this real?"

Instead of an answer, he put a hand on my shoulder. My skin felt hot where he touched me. Tingles ran down my spine.

"Do you feel the connection?" he asked softly. "Are you ready to accept it?"

Was I ready? I'd spent a week fighting it. The idea

of having a predetermined soulmate went against all my principles of self-determination, but at the same time, I couldn't deny that there was *something* between us.

"Yes," I admitted. "I feel it. I'm not sure I want to, but I do."

An'tia whinnied from behind us. Matchmaker *and* cheerleader. Our stabhorn was multi-talented.

Bruin moved his hand to my cheek, but it was only the faintest touch, as if he was scared of my reaction. I leaned into his touch, revelling in how soft his palm felt against my cheek.

"I would like to kiss you," he whispered hoarsely.

I looked him straight in the eyes. My mind was made up. "Then do it."

He moved faster than I could process. He wrapped one arm around my waist, pulling me close, then his lips crushed onto mine, hard yet supple. For a moment, I felt as if I was lifted out of my body. I floated above us, a golden tether connecting me to my body. And not just to mine. A second tether, a thin line of silver, led right into Bruin's chest. Instinctively I knew that this strand would grow stronger over time until our bond was permanent. And to my surprise, I was looking forward to it. It felt right. I wanted to be connected to him. I recognised something familiar within him, something that had almost made me feel different from everybody else.

His hand tangled my hair, steadying my head as

our lips moved in sync. His earthy scent hit me and I was pulled back into my body. Our eyes met and I knew everything was going to be alright.

# LESSON 11

# XERVEN TRADITIONS 201

# LESSON 11: XERVEN TRADITIONS 201

BRUIN

She fit into my arms perfectly. Her lips, so soft and gentle, moulded against mine. I knew deep within my heart that this was meant to be. We'd been raised a galaxy apart, but we'd always been meant to be together. We were two halves of a whole and for the first time in my life, I felt complete. Pure joy filled my soul. I wanted to scream with happiness. Tara was mine, my mate, my female, my queen. Holding her in my arms was the best feeling in the universe.

I deepened the kiss and she opened her lips willingly, letting me in. I playfully swiped my tongue against hers before claiming her mouth. I'd been holding back for so long, but now I was letting go. I gave myself to her. Poured all my pent-up emotions into our kiss. Showed her just how much she meant to me.

I don't know how long we stood like that, our

breaths mingling, our bodies entwined. We were one. How it was supposed to be.

Her hands roamed over my back, slipping under my tunic. Shivers ran down my skin and straight into my cocks. I was harder than ever before. My mating cock pulsed within its sleeve, begging to be released. Soon. I'd not explained the starlight ritual to her yet. Was she ready? I hoped she was.

When we finally broke apart, we were both breathing hard. Her cheeks were flushed, her lips bright red, her pupils wide. I wanted to kiss her again right away. My mate was the prettiest female in the universe. And she was mine.

An'tia snorted impatiently, as if to say, get a room. I smirked, amused by the stabhorn's manipulation. She'd get extra treats after we'd completed the ritual. She was manipulating and arrogant, a true diva, but without her, I would never have found Tara.

I returned my attention to my mate. A smile played around her swollen lips. She looked happier than I'd ever seen her. For a moment, I was sad that she'd been unable to be this happy for the first week of our journey. I should have handled it all differently. Maybe if I'd figured out An'tia's manipulation earlier, it wouldn't have been as hard for Tara. But it was too late to change the past. All I could do was ensure that she'd have the happiest future imaginable.

"Thank you," I said, my voice hoarse with emotion.

"For what?"

"For trusting me. For letting go of your doubts. For giving me the best kiss I've ever had."

She quirked an eyebrow. "The best, huh? I think we can top that."

She put her hands on my hips, pulling me closer. Amused, I leaned down and kissed her once again. Talks about the ritual could wait.

An'tia's impatient whinnies ended our kiss. She was hungry. Tara and I worked together to fill her trough and make sure she had enough water.

"Let's give her some time alone," Tara said with a grin. I bet she wasn't suggesting that just for the stabhorn's sake. As tempted as I was to take her right into my bedroom and start the ritual, I didn't want to rush her. Instead, we headed to the relaxation quarter. I ordered two kiki shakes from Andromeda and they appeared on the table a few clicks later.

"What's that?" Tara asked when I handed her a glass.

"Kiki shakes, a delicacy from planet Kardar. I don't know what they're made from, probably better not to know. But they're delicious. Try it."

She gave the murky grey liquid a questioning look, but then took a cautious sip. I watched with pleasure as her eyes widened and her eyebrows shot up. Her face was so expressive.

"That's delicious," she moaned and drained the glass with a few large gulps. "Can I have another?"

With a grin, I passed her demand on to Andromeda. I sipped my shake slowly, my attention fully focused on my mate. I loved seeing her this happy and relaxed. She finished her second shake before I emptied my glass. I made a mental note to provide her with daily shakes. They were full of essential vitamins and minerals. Essential for Xervens, but maybe for Peritans as well. I would have to look it up. Andromeda had strict instructions to only serve food and drinks suitable for Peritans, but I hadn't researched if the same things were healthy for the both of us. It would be strange if Xerven junk food turned out to be nutritious for Tara.

We sat down on one of the benches, our thighs touching. I didn't even mind that the bench was uncomfortable because it wasn't made for my tall frame.

"I would like to talk about the starlight ritual," I said and took her hand. She didn't pull away. On the contrary, she leaned against my side and rested her head on my shoulder. I had to crouch to let her do that, but I'd take the discomfort to make her happy.

"What is it?" she asked. Her voice was so lovely when she wasn't screaming at me.

"The ritual will cement the mating bond between us. It will give you the same legal rights on Allopo that I have, but it will also... How do I put this without sounding crude?"

"Just spit it out," she encouraged, using one of her strange expressions. I wasn't going to spit on her.

"How many cocks do Peritan males have?" I blurted. I'd forgotten to check.

Tara looked at me as if I'd grown Ferven horns. "One. What are you saying? You have more than one?"

Her gaze flicked to my crotch, but she caught herself quickly and focused back on my face. I imagined how she was fighting the temptation to look back at my trousers, which felt way too tight by now.

"I have two," I confirmed. "One is my pleasure cock, which has been active ever since I reached maturity. The other is my mating cock, trapped in a sleeve until my mate releases it during the starlight ritual. Only the mating cock can pass on my seed to a female. And my mate is the only one who will ever get to feel both my cocks inside of her."

Tara sucked in a sharp breath. "Both? At the same time?"

"Of course. I have been told it is even more pleasurable for the female than it is for the male."

Again, she couldn't resist peeking at my crotch. "How does that work? I don't know what Xerven women look like down below, but I doubt there's space for two dicks inside me. Unless they're tiny. Wait, what size - no, never mind." Her cheeks reddened again. Adorable.

"They will fit," I reassured her. "My mating cock will change shape to match your physiology. It's why Xervens can find mates among other species. We're...flexible."

Tara giggled. "You don't want to know what I'm

thinking just now. But that means your, what did you call it, pleasure cock can't make a woman pregnant?"

"It cannot. It is only there to help a male gather experience which will in turn help him pleasure his future mate properly. But nobody has ever seen or touched my mating cock, not even I. It is for you alone."

"That's almost romantic, if a little weird." She laughed again. "So what does that ritual entail?"

"Usually, the couple's family will attend, but I don't want my sire to be part of it and your family-"

"I don't have one," she interrupted brusquely.

I'd noticed that she'd never mentioned wanting to return to her family during our fights, only her home. It had made me realise her family was either dead or estranged from her. One day, I'd ask her, but I didn't want to ruin the mood. Not now that we were so close to becoming permanent mates.

"We will do the ritual together, just us," I continued. "Unless you want An'tia to watch."

Tara's wide grin returned. "No way."

"I agree. We will both cleanse ourselves, then present our naked bodies to each other. It signifies openness and trust. There are some old Xerven words we have to say, but you can simply follow my lead. Then you remove the sleeve of my mating cock and-"

"Wait," she interrupted. "This is terribly unromantic. I don't want to hear all of it in advance. It might put me off going through with it. Right now, I'm crazy enough to do your ritual. I should probably wait and take off my rose-tinted glasses, but fuck it. If An'tia thinks we're to be together, then so be it. It's not like I have anything waiting for me on Earth. I always wanted to travel. And we won't have to stay on your planet all the time, right? We can visit my friends. Who probably believe I'm dead by now. Maybe not such a good idea. I should-"

I put a finger on her lips, silencing her. "Yes. We can go wherever you want. Once my sire determines that I have completed the job, I will be paid and will have the resources to give you the life you deserve."

"I will find some sort of job," Tara promised. "I don't want to be a lone little housewife. I don't know what I'll be able to do on your planet, but I definitely won't sit at home all day, waiting for you to come home."

"I never expected you to stay at home," I said quickly. "You could start as my apprentice, working with stabhorns. You're so good with An'tia that I don't think it'll take long for you to learn how to care for other stabhorns. We could make a business out of it. Our own stabhorn park."

Tara shot me one of her beautiful smiles. "I like that. As long as none of them try to matchmake again. I don't want to be stabbed."

I laughed. "After the starlight ritual, even the most stubborn stabhorn will know that we're together. There will never be another female in my life. Never. You're the one, Tara Crawford. Are you ready for the ritual?"

She bit her bottom lip. With every click that passed in silence, my heart grew heavier, until she finally nodded. "Yes. I'm ready."

# LESSON 12

# ADVANCED MATING TECHNIQUES

# LESSON 12: ADVANCED MATING
# TECHNIQUES

TARA

Alone in the shower room, doubts flooded in at the same time as the cleansing fog covered my body. Was I rushing into something? What if I never came to love Bruin? Right now, I liked him, a lot, despite all his mistakes and blunders, but it wasn't love. At least it couldn't be, not after a week. Right? That flutter in my belly when I thought of him was just nerves about the ritual. It wasn't more than that. Love was something that happened over time, not the moment you met. Instant love was reserved for books and films, not reality. But the thought of not being with him hurt. It was strange how quickly it had all changed. Yet it felt right. Natural.

I ran my hands over my body, once again wishing I had a sponge or cloth. I wanted to be squeaky clean for Bruin. I had no razor either, but I rarely bothered shaving back home. I wouldn't start with it now. I shouldn't want to change my habits for Bruin. He'd have to accept me with some fluff included.

Once the fog in the shower room disappeared, I hesitated. It was only Bruin and me on the ship, but I also didn't want to walk around naked.

"Andromeda, I need a robe."

A cupboard door appeared on one wall that had been smooth a second ago. I opened it to find a long purple robe made from a silky material. The purple was almost the shade of Bruin's skin. Just like all the clothes the ship had provided, it fit me perfectly. Feeling more confident with the robe covering my body, I stepped out of the shower room. The corridor was dimly lit like it always was at night, even though it was only late afternoon. Bright flecks of light on the floor led the way.

"Stars," I muttered to myself and followed the trail to Bruin's bedroom. I'd not been inside it before; the only room in the entire spaceship I hadn't explored. My heart was beating fast. This was the moment. I lifted a hand to knock, but the door slid open, revealing a large chamber four times as big as my own bedroom. The only furniture was a huge bed in the centre. A shiny indigo sheet covered the mattress. And in the centre of the bed stood Bruin, fully naked, his cock hard and erect, his arms outstretched.

Oh my, his dick was huge. That would never fit. I noticed a lack of balls, but then forced myself to look away. I focused on his chest instead. Chiselled abs, smooth skin, a nipple-less chest. Not a single hair anywhere, confirming my theory that Xervens - or at least Bruin - didn't have body hair. He had no belly button, but that only highlighted the tense muscles that looked as if carved from stone. He was gorgeous, perfect and slightly intimidating. What would he think of me? I was nothing like him. I had love handles, a belly that sometimes got in the way, and boobs that were droopier than I liked. The right was slightly bigger than the left, which meant no bra ever fit properly. And I had a large mole on my right collarbone that I'd always wanted to get removed. In short, I didn't look like a model. Not like Bruin.

"Take off your robe," he said hoarsely. "And join me."

I realised he'd been checking me out just like I had been. Except that he'd been hindered by the robe. I hesitated for a moment, but then assembled my courage and let the robe drop to the floor. I locked eyes with him, pretending I was confident in my skin, and stepped onto the bed. The mattress hardened beneath my feet. Alien technology, no doubt.

Bruin kept my gaze trapped in his, never looking at my naked body. I was grateful.

When I reached him, he wrapped his strong arms around me, pulling me into a tight embrace. His hard cock pressed against my belly, while my boobs got squashed between us. My nipples were almost as hard as his cock by now. My core tingled with need. How long had it been since I'd last slept with a guy? I couldn't even remember. And it had meant nothing. Just a quick fuck to take care of my needs. This was different. This was my mate.

"You're beautiful," he whispered, his lips only a breath away from mine. His voice was husky, which turned me on immensely. He sounded like sex.

"So are you."

He smiled, his eyes sparkling with joy. "I can't believe this is happening. I never thought I'd get to do the starlight ritual. Bind myself to my mate forever."

Forever. A shiver ran down my back. That was a long time. But I wouldn't turn back now.

Bruin kissed me ever so softly, then stepped back. I instantly felt cold, bereft of his warmth. I wanted to be in his arms again.

"Speak after me. Your implant doesn't translate Old Xerven, so I am going to say the words in the modern dialect. They won't rhyme and won't sound as beautiful, but I want you to understand what you're repeating."

I bowed my head in thanks. He was so thoughtful.

He went onto his knees, looking up at me with awe. I motioned to do the same, but he stopped me. For a moment, I thought he'd propose to me, then remembered he wouldn't know what that was.

"'Tara Crawford, of Peritus, the stars have led me to you. From now on, they will guide us together, through light and dark. I pledge my light to you. I pledge my darkness to you. I will be your guiding star when you need it. I will follow your light when I'm in the dark. We will shine together forevermore."

Shivers ran down my back and my eyes stung. His words were so beautiful and I knew he meant every single one. His eyes blazed with emotion as he held out his hands. I grasped them tightly, grateful to have something to hold onto.

"I, Bruin, son of Tholin, of Allopo, accept you as my mate."

He didn't have to encourage me to speak.

"I, Tara Crawford, of Peritus, accept you as my mate."

He squeezed my hands in approval. "I will serve your light until the day it flickers out."

I repeated his words solemnly, my voice shaking slightly. I felt like I was in a dream, yet at the same time, his touch kept me grounded in reality.

"I will protect, encourage and strengthen your light."

I took a deep breath. "I will protect, encourage and strengthen your light."

Bruin got back to his feet but kept my hands in his. "And now we shall bring our lights together to burn brighter than ever before."

He pulled me into his arms. I clung to him, tears now freely streaming down my cheeks. Tears of joy. I'd never felt happier. For a second, I could see the tether between us, no longer just a thin silver band, but now a braid of silver and gold, glowing brightly. Then my vision cleared, but I didn't doubt what I had seen was real. There really was a bond between us.

I rose on my tiptoes and kissed him. It likely wasn't the right thing to do at this stage of the ritual, but I had to. I needed to feel his lips bruising mine. I'd thought the kiss in the hangar had been special. It was nothing compared to this. Our tongues danced, our breaths became one. I was dimly aware of his hardness, of my own arousal. I reached between us, took his cock into my hand. His skin was hot, much warmer than the rest of his body.

Bruin groaned, a sound that spurred me on. I broke the kiss with one last nibble on his bottom lip, then dropped to my knees. His cock stood proud right before me, but I was curious in the bulge underneath. Instead of balls, he had one large mound behind the base of his cock. I ran my fingers over it, eliciting a string of curses from Bruin. So he liked that. Good. I kissed the tip of his huge purple cock, then tried to take him into my mouth. I barely managed to get my lips wrapped around him. His breathing was loud and hard. Music to my ears. I loved having this effect on him. When I swiped my tongue against his engorged tip, he jerked in my mouth.

"How are you doing that?" Bruin groaned. "How can this feel so good?"

I stroked the bulge again, careful not to scratch the sensitive skin. A strange tingle flashed through my wet pussy, as if I'd touched myself. I did it again, and once more it felt as if by stroking the bulge, I also flicked my own clit. Wow. Talk about a bond between mates. When I did it a third time, Bruin gripped my hair as if he needed something to hold on to. You and me both, dear. I was glad I was on my knees.

"You need to get my mating cock out before I explode," he huffed, breathing hard.

I leaned my head back and his cock flopped from my lips. "How?"

"There's a slit underneath. Lick it."

I felt for the slit. A thin line, like a scar, ran along the base of the bulge where it curved towards his arse. Without hesitation, I lowered myself between his legs and licked along the slit.

Bruin roared. That was all the warning I got. Suddenly his hands were clasped around my shoulders and then I was flung back onto the bed. It turned soft the moment my back hit the sheet, welcoming me into its warmth. Bruin towered above me, a mountain of a man, now with two cocks, one above the other. His mating dick was slightly smaller, but for human standards, he was still more than well endowed. I felt more confident about being able to take that one. He spread my legs, then kneeled between them, his cocks pointing right at my pussy. I was dripping wet and my core was throbbing with desire. I didn't want foreplay. I needed him to fuck me right now.

"Take me," I begged, but it turned into a moan. "Claim me."

Fire burned in his dark eyes, a smouldering heat that signalled the things to come. I couldn't wait. He positioned his lower cock so his tip pressed against my entrance. The other cock pushed along my folds, rubbing against my clit. I wouldn't have needed the extra stimulation but wow, I could already see how amazing it would be to have one of his cocks inside me while the other provided extra stimulation.

"Are you ready?" he asked huskily.

I sunk my fingers into the soft mattress, clinging to the sheet for support. "I'm ready."

He needed no further encouragement. He pushed into me with one smooth motion. I gasped as he filled me to the brink, stretching me almost to the point it hurt. My pussy clenched around him. He gave me a moment to adjust to his girth, but he used it to cup my breasts, squeezing my nipples, making me moan with desire. His every touch sent fire through my body and into my core. I was burning for him and only he could douse the flames.

He pulled out, leaving me feeling bereft for a heartbeat, then he pushed in again, hard and fast. I welcomed him. This was what I needed. I craved to be fucked into oblivion, claimed as his mate. He set a rapid pace that no human would have been able to keep up for long. His pleasure cock rubbed over my clit, driving me crazy with every touch. Our moans became a chorus of ecstasy as he drove us higher and higher until there was no way back. I shattered, exploding into a million pieces, but his light held them together, gathered them up and reassembled them into a new person. I did the same for him, binding him to me as my alien mate.

We slowly floated back into reality, but only to rise once more, his stamina unchallenged, and a third time, until I was drenched in sweat and too exhausted to move. He held me in his arms, whispered sweet words of love, and I knew that I had finally found what I'd been looking for all my life.

# FINAL ASSIGNMENT

# HAPPILY EVER AFTER

# FINAL ASSIGNMENT: HAPPILY EVER
# AFTER

## Two years later

BRUIN

The stabhorn fowl rose on unsteady legs, its huge blue eyes searching for its mother. An'tia licked the newborn's wet forehead, her tongue circling the tiny stub that would once grow into a horn. Her mate, a proud stallion named Gwain, stood nearby, watching over his young family. He was Tara's favourite, the first stabhorn she'd tamed on her own. She was a natural when it came to caring for our herd. We had fifteen stabhorns now with An'tia as their matriarch. It had been a surprise to all of us when she'd fallen pregnant. She was young to be a mother, but she made up for it with maturity and confidence.

"She's gorgeous," Tara cooed. "Or is it a boy?"

"It's a female," I confirmed and looked down at my

mate. Her eyes were glowing with excitement. The second sun was about to set, my favourite time of the day. The pre-evening light turned Tara's blonde hair into molten gold, a reminder of the time I'd first dreamed of her.

An'tia snorted, telling us to back off. It was her time to be a mother.

I checked my scanner, making sure the fowl's vitals were normal, before taking my mate's hand and leading her away from the birthing paddock.

"She'll make a great mum," Tara said happily. "And Gwain will be a good father once he learns to be less self-obsessed."

"Sirehood will be good for him," I agreed. "His arrogance is only bluster. I think deep inside, he's not as confident as he lets on."

Like myself, before I'd met my mate. I'd been lost, drifting without a destination. She'd shown me the way to true happiness. Every day with her was a miracle. I still marvelled how I deserved her by my side.

Tara had quickly got used to life on Allopo. She'd started as my apprentice with both of us working for my old boss, but she'd learned fast. After half a rotation, we'd left and started our own stabhorn herd. My sire had not been happy until Tara had volunteered to send him regular updates on her relationship with An'tia. He'd published his research on Peritan beliefs and got some kind of award for it, which had placated him somewhat. He no longer tried to persuade me to work for the IGU. In his own way, he may have finally understood that I wasn't completely useless - not that he'd ever admit to that. But his jibes and taunts had become less since he'd met Tara.

"I don't think I'll ever get used to having two suns," Tara muttered.

She leaned against my chest, watching the sunset like we did every evening. The second sun was dipping beneath the hills in the distance, while the first sun was racing across the sky to catch up with her sister. The sky was about to turn from a golden orange into a deep red. The temperature would drop rapidly, although now, in summer, it wouldn't get cold enough to need a coat.

I wrapped my arms around my mate, lending her some of my warmth. She hated being cold, which was funny considering how often it rained in the country she'd grown up in. The bulge under her purple dress was starting to get noticeable. The little stabhorn wouldn't be the only fowl in our herd for long. I placed my hands on her stomach, imagining the life growing within. We'd created that life, together. We'd be a family soon. As so often since I'd found out we were expecting offspring, I imagined what they would look like. Would they have Tara's pink complexion or my own purple skin? Would they have hair? I hoped so. I loved running my fingers through Tara's golden locks, braiding them like I braided stabhorn manes. I imagined a herd of younglings, all with braided hair, and Tara and me in their centre.

"You're smiling," Tara said without turning around.

"I love that I know that."

The mating bond between us was growing stronger every day. Sometimes, I knew what Tara was about to say before she opened her mouth. We could sense each other's feelings, even at a distance. And now she could feel my smile.

"Do you know what I'm doing now?" I asked and pursed my lips as if I was kissing her. I even wiggled my tongue for good measure.

"I can." She turned around with a soft laugh. "And I'm jealous of the air you just kissed."

"The air has nothing on you, sweet mate." I lifted her into my arms, pressing her against my chest. Tara quickly wrapped her legs around my hips before our lips met in a passionate kiss. She tasted like starlight.

In the distance, An'tia whinnied with joy.

I knew exactly how she felt.

I hope you enjoyed Alien Abduction for Unicorns!

This is only one of many stories set in the Starlight Universe. For more, take a look at *The Intergalactic Guide to Humans*: https://skyemackinnon.com/ intergalactic-guide.html

Get the first book for free by subscribing to Skye's newsletter: https://books.skyemackinnon.com/ lbf90329z7

## AFTERWORD

Dear readers,

First of all, let me apologise to all tourists. You really aren't as bad as Tara made you out to be.

I worked in Scottish tourism for two years and it was one of the best jobs I've ever had (besides being an author, obviously). Interacting with people from around the world and answering their questions was great fun and certainly never got boring.

If you've been wondering where Tara worked, it's Stirling Castle.

I went to university in Stirling and thought it was high time that I set a story there, even if it's just for a chapter. Sadly, I never got abducted by aliens during the five years I lived in one of Scotland's most beautiful cities, nor did I ever meet a real unicorn. Still, I highly recommend you visit if you're ever in the area.

One of the other reasons why I chose Stirling Castle as Tara's workplace is because it is home to the famous <u>Stirling Tapestries</u>, hand-woven works of art depicting the Hunt of the Unicorn. It took fourteen years for the seven tapestries to be completed and visitors got to watch the weavers work in their workshop at the castle. I went there many times, fascinated by how they were bringing this ancient story to life. But the tapestries aren't the only place where you can find unicorns at Stirling Castle. Because the unicorn is Scotland's national animal (and until 1603, the Royal Coat of Arms of Scotland featured two unicorns, before it got changed to a lion and a unicorn), they're <u>everywhere</u> - painted on walls, immortalised in stone statues, carved into wooden decorations.

If you're ever in the area, I highly recommend a visit.


A big thank you to my fellow Flockers Arizona Tape, Laura Greenwood and Bea Paige for all the motivation, sprints and pep talks. I wrote this story while feeling very stressed about a house move, but as always my friends were there for moral support. Unicorn sparkles for all of you!

Happy reading,
Skye

## COULD YOU ABDUCT A HUMAN?

Do you think you've got what it takes to become an alien abductor? Take this test to find out!

**hi.switchy.io/AAFBtest**

*(if you share your results on social media, be sure to tag me)*

And if you feel like you've passed this course, you can download a certificate!

**hi.switchy.io/AAFBcertificate**

# THE INTERGALACTIC GUIDE TO HUMANS

Abductions aren't easy - which is exactly why the Intergalactic University offers a range of courses at various levels. Immerse yourself in this strange, comical universe and work on your abduction skills.

Find all books in this series here:
skyemackinnon.com/intergalactic-guide

Alien Abduction for Beginners
Alien Abduction for Professionals
Alien Abduction for Experts

Alien Abduction for Santa

Alien Abduction for Pirates

Alien Abduction for Milkmen

Alien Abduction for Unicorns

# ABOUT THE AUTHOR

Skye MacKinnon is a USA Today & International Bestselling Author whose books are filled with strong heroines who don't have to choose.

She embraces her Scottishness with fantastical Scottish settings and a dash of mythology, no matter if she's writing about Celtic gods, aliens, cat shifters, or the streets of Edinburgh.

When she's not typing away at her favourite cafe, Skye loves dried mango, as much exotic tea as she can squeeze into her cupboards, and being covered in pet hair by her tiny black cat.

Subscribe to her newsletter:
**skyemackinnon.com/newsletter**

Find all of Skye's sci-fi romance in one place:
**skyemackinnon.com/scifi**

# THE STARLIGHT UNIVERSE

*This book is part of the Starlight Universe, an entire galaxy filled with hunky aliens, exotic planets, and the human women ready to find love among the stars.*

## Starlight Highlanders Mail Order Brides

Alien Highlanders in kilts come to Earth in search of brides... and take them to planet Albya. Three m/f standalones full of humour, action and steamy romance. Part of the Intergalactic Dating Agency.

## The Intergalactic Guide to Humans

A humorous take on alien abductions, probing and other shenanigans. One reverse harem trilogy about clueless aliens and the human woman they abducted, followed by several standalone romances with various pairings (m/f, f/m/f and m/m). If you want light entertainment filled with unicorns, fabulous misunderstandings and unusual body parts, this is the series for you.

## Starlight Vikings

Set on Earth and on the spaceship Valkyr, this trilogy of m/f standalones is all about hunky alien Vikings in need of females. Part of the Intergalactic Dating Agency.

## Starlight Monsters

These aliens are not your usual humanoids... they have claws, fangs, tails, scales, knotty dicks and will growl at you. Interconnected m/f standalones with lots of action, steam and fated mates.

# ALSO BY

Find all of Skye's books on her website, skyemackinnon.com, where you can also order signed paperbacks and swag.

Many of her books are available as audiobooks.

## SCIENCE FICTION ROMANCE

### Set in the Starlight Universe

- **Starlight Vikings** (sci-fi m/f romance, part of the Intergalactic Dating Agency)
- **Starlight Monsters** (sci-fi m/f romance)
- **Starlight Highlanders Mail Order Brides** (sci-fi m/f romance, part of the Intergalactic Dating Agency)
- **The Intergalactic Guide to Humans** (sci-fi romance with various pairings)

### Set in other worlds

- **Between Rebels** (sci-fi reverse harem set in the Planet Athion shared world)
- **The Mars Diaries** (sci-fi reverse harem)

- **Aliens and Animals** (f/f sci-fi romance co-written with Arizona Tape)
- **Through the Gates** (dystopian reverse harem co-written with Rebecca Royce)

PARANORMAL & FANTASY ROMANCE

- **Claiming Her Bears** (post-apocalyptic shifter reverse harem)
- **Daughter of Winter** (fantasy reverse harem)
- **Catnip Assassins** (urban fantasy reverse harem)
- **Infernal Descent** (paranormal reverse harem based on Dante's Inferno, co-written with Bea Paige)
- **Seven Wardens** (fantasy reverse harem co-written with Laura Greenwood)
- **The Lost Siren** (post-apocalyptic, paranormal reverse harem co-written with Liza Street)

OTHER SERIES

- **Academy of Time** (time travel academy standalones, reverse harem and m/f)
- **Defiance** (contemporary reverse harem with a hint of thriller/suspense)

STANDALONES

- Song of Souls – m/f fantasy romance, fairy tale retelling
- Their Hybrid – steampunk reverse harem
- Partridge in the P.E.A.R. - sci-fi reverse harem co-written with Arizona Tape
- Highland Butterflies – lesbian romance

ANTHOLOGIES AND BOX SETS

- Hungry for More – charity cookbook
- Daggers & Destiny – a Skye MacKinnon starter library

# NOTES

## A NOTE ON UNICORNS

1. *For some reason, Peritans have not adopted the intergalactic standard name for their planet yet.*

CPSIA information can be obtained
at www.ICGtesting.com
Printed in the USA
BVHW032307010323
659544BV00003B/10

9 798215 717134